FLAMES OVER FRANCE

* available from Severn House

FLAMES
OVER FRANCE

Robert Jackson

This first world edition published in Great Britain 1997 by
SEVERN HOUSE PUBLISHERS LTD of
9–15 High Street, Sutton, Surrey SM1 1DF.
First published in the USA 1997 by
SEVERN HOUSE PUBLISHERS INC., of
595 Madison Avenue, New York, NY 10022.

British Library Cataloguing in Publication Data
Jackson, Robert, 1941–
    Flames over France
    1.English fiction – 20th century
    I.Title
    823.9'14[F]

    ISBN 0-7278-5196-9

Typeset by Hewer Text Composition Services, Edinburgh.
Printed and bound in Great Britain by
Hartnolls Ltd, Bodmin, Cornwall.

Prelude: Dawn, 10 May 1940

The inhabitants of the villages dotted over the countryside west of Cologne stirred fitfully in their sleep, disturbed by the rumble in the eastern sky. The noise grew louder, swelling to a crescendo that rattled tiles and window panes. Hands fumbled with blackout curtains, heavy eyes peering up into the pre-dawn light, but the silhouettes of the aircraft were lost against the fading stars. The armada thundered on, heading due west, and silence returned to the land bordering the Rhine.

It was 0345. Twenty minutes earlier, the forty-one Junkers Ju 52 three-engined transports now droning westwards had taken off at thirty-second intervals from the airfields of Butzweilerhof and Ostheim, on opposite banks of the Rhine near Cologne. Each Ju 52 towed a DFS 230 heavy assault glider, laden with troops and equipment. Navigation for the transport crews was simple: they followed a line of flashing ground beacons, stretching all the way to Aachen.

Beyond Aachen, along the frontiers of Belgium and Holland, the massed divisions of the *Wehrmacht* were poised, steel spearheads ready to thrust deep into the Low Countries.

On the hard benches in the swaying gliders, the men of Assault Detachment Koch sat tensely as the minutes ticked by. For six months they had trained for this mission, six months during which each man had learned how to perform his individual task blindfold. They were elite troops, these men, and proud of their status. Moreover, they all knew that the outcome of this initial phase of

1

the invasion depended on them. They were to strike the first blow.

The forty-one gliders were split up into four waves, each with its own specific target. The first, known as Storm Group Granite and consisting of eleven gliders carrying a total of eighty-five men, was to descend on the Belgian fortress of Eben Emael, a formidable strongpoint commanding the Albert Canal south of Maastricht. The second, Storm Group Concrete, with ninety-six men in eleven gliders, was to capture the bridge over the Maas at Vroenhoven and prevent its destruction by the defenders. The third, Storm Group Steel, had as its objective the bridge at Veldwezelt, over the Albert Canal north of Vroenhoven; Steel consisted of nine gliders carrying ninety-two men. The third bridge over the canal, at Kanne, was the target of the ten gliders and ninety soldiers of Storm Group Iron.

The outward flight was not without incident. Trouble hit Storm Group Granite shortly after take-off when the pilot of the eleventh and last Junkers in this wave suddenly saw the blue exhaust flames of another aircraft ahead and to starboard, very close and on a converging course. To avoid a collision the pilot pushed the Junkers into a dive. In the glider behind, the pilot desperately tried to follow the sudden manoeuvre. He was not quick enough; there was a sudden jolt as the tow-rope parted under the strain. The glider pilot turned back and landed in a meadow near Cologne.

Aboard the glider was *Oberleutnant* Rudolf Witzig, the commander of Storm Group Granite. While his men worked like slaves to turn the meadow into a landing-strip, he unpacked his collapsible bicycle and pedalled off down the road. A passing motorist gave him a lift and he was back at Ostheim twenty minutes later, telling his story to the duty officer. All Ostheim's Junkers were airborne on the mission and a replacement aircraft had to be sent through from Gutersloh. While the duty officer was on the telephone, Witzig looked fretfully at his watch. It was 0410;

2

another fifteen minutes and the others would be going down on their targets.

Meanwhile, the other forty Ju 52s, each towing its glider, droned on towards the frontier. Then came another mishap. The pilot of a second glider in Storm Group Granite saw – or thought he saw – his towing aircraft flash the signal to cast off. He pulled the yellow handle and the tow-rope dropped away. The glider, not yet halfway to the frontier, came down in a field near Duren and the men made their way in commandeered cars to join the *Wehrmacht* units poised for the main assault.

The rest of the force flew on. Because of the rigid radio silence, the other members of Storm Group Granite were not yet aware that their numbers had been seriously depleted. Ahead of them now, in the distance, a lone searchlight probed upward; it was a marker and at its base lay Aachen. The Junkers had been climbing steadily all the way, and by the time they reached that last beacon their altitude would be 8,000 feet. Another fifteen minutes and they would be over the junction of the Dutch, Belgian and German borders; then the Junkers would turn away and the gliders would swoop silently towards their objectives.

On the other side of the Albert Canal, the defenders of Fort Eben Emael – the Belgian 7th Infantry Regiment – had been on the alert since 0200, peering into the darkness shrouding the fourteen-mile strip of Dutch territory that separated Belgium from Germany at this point. The men of the 7th Infantry were confident that they could withstand even the strongest assault. Eben Emael was the most impenetrable fortress in the world. Sited on a plateau on the west bank of the Albert Canal, the fort measured 1,000 yards long by 700 yards wide at its broadest part. On its north-eastern flank, the fortress ended in a sheer 130-foot drop into the canal. Its other flanks were protected by wide anti-tank ditches, which in turn were covered by blockhouses mounting searchlights, heavy machine-guns and anti-tank weapons. Inside the perimeter, heavily reinforced concrete and metal bunkers covered every inch of the ground with their field of fire. Any assailants who managed to get across the ditches would be caught in the deadly crossfire of weapons, with calibres ranging from the .5-inch of the machine-guns to the 3-inch muzzles of the artillery.

The designers of the fortress of Eben Emael had proudly claimed that it was invulnerable to attack. So it was, by the standards of the 1914–18 war. But its designers had overlooked, or perhaps disregarded, one eventuality: an attack from the air. As an afterthought, one light anti-aircraft battery had been positioned near the fort's south-east corner. And that was all.

At about 0420, there was a sudden alert as a flurry of anti-aircraft shellbursts twinkled across the sky in the direction of Maastricht. The fire was directed against the Ju 52s, which had just released their gliders and which were now dropping parachutes, each carrying a dummy festooned with firecrackers, to confuse the Belgians. The garrison of Eben Emael, believing the anti-aircraft fire to be a signal that German bombers were crossing the frontier, strained their ears to catch the sound of aero-engines; they heard nothing and relaxed a little.

Suddenly, a black shadow swept in low from the east, accompanied by a peculiar whining noise. It dropped down between two blockhouses and slid to a stop on a patch of clear ground, a hundred yards from a machine-gun bunker. The Belgian gunners strove frantically to depress and traverse the barrels of their weapons as more gliders touched down. Soldiers burst from the first glider and fanned out towards their objective, Bunker No. 19. A machine-gun stuttered, firing blindly. A German NCO crouched by the bunker wall and dropped a satchel of high explosive through the periscope slit in the armoured dome. There was the dull thud of an explosion and the chatter of the machine-gun stopped abruptly.

A burst of gunfire came from the southern corner of the fort; tracers lanced out into the half-light and three German soldiers fell. The rest went into action and laid an explosive charge against the wall of the bunker. A moment later the stunned and deafened defenders staggered out into the open through the shattered cupola, their hands on their heads.

Within ten minutes, as many bunkers had been destroyed. However, by this time the Belgians had realised that the attacking force consisted of only seventy-odd men. The garrison commander rang the CO of a nearby artillery battery and asked him to lay down a barrage on the fort itself. Soon, the earth was erupting among the abandoned gliders and the attackers themselves were forced to seek shelter in the shattered bunkers. Reeling under the impact of the artillery barrage the Germans prepared to fight it out, holding on if possible until the main *Wehrmacht* thrust reached the canal.

For three hours, a pitched battle raged under the drifting smoke that obscured Eben Emael. Then, at 0730, the unexpected happened; a glider winged in through the smoke and rumbled to a stop near the wreckage of Bunker No. 19. It was Rudolf Witzig and his men, who had at last reached the battle after being pulled out of the meadow near Cologne by the Junkers from Gutersloh. Witzig took command from *Feldwebel* Wenzel, who as senior NCO had been directing operations so far in the absence of any officers.

A few minutes later, a flight of Heinkel He 111 bombers roared overhead and dropped several containers of ammunition to the German sappers, who renewed their attack on the remaining bunkers. Hour after hour the battle swayed to and fro, with the Belgians fighting stubbornly for every square foot of ground. At last, Witzig managed to establish radio contact with Storm Groups Concrete and Iron at Vroenhoven and Kanne; the news he received was not good. It appeared that the bridges in Maastricht itself had been destroyed by the defenders and the one at Kanne, which linked Maastricht with Eben Emael, had been blown up just as the assault gliders touched down. However, the main bridges at Vroenhoven and Weldwezelt had been captured intact, and across them the *Panzer* divisions were flooding into the Low Countries.

All that day and all the next night, Storm Group Granite clung doggedly to its foothold in Eben Emael, with the help of air support from German dive-bombers, Junkers Ju 87 *Stukas* and Henschel Hs 123 biplanes. Finally, at 0700 on 11 May, the weary, unshaven soldiers were relieved by shock troops, who proceeded to wipe out all remaining resistance. By noon, it was all over. In the clear sunshine, under a sky dappled with cirrus cloud, the haggard, uncomprehending Belgian soldiers – 1,200 of them – threw down their weapons and marched into captivity under the sub-machine guns of the victors. Eben Emael had fallen and the way was now open for the armoured spearheads of General Fedor von Bock's Army Group B, spreading out across the drab Belgian plain west of the Meuse.

As the battle for Eben Emael moved towards its climax in the gathering daylight, twenty-eight Heinkels of *Kampfgeschwader* 4 thundered inland over the Hook of Holland. They had taken off from their bases at Gutersloh, Fassberg and Delmenhorst at 0500 and were now approaching their target: the airport of Waalhaven, on the outskirts of Rotterdam.

In an attempt to confuse the Dutch defences the bomber formation had made a wide detour around northern Holland and was now making its run-in from the west, from the direction of the British Isles. But the Dutch were wide awake; as the bombers crossed the coast they ran into heavy flak, and a few seconds later they were attacked by Fokker D.21 fighters of the 2nd Air Regiment, Netherlands Army Air Force. The leading Heinkel went down with both engines on fire; the crew bailed out.

The remaining bombers droned on towards Waalhaven. In Rotterdam, the air raid sirens were howling full blast. Simultaneously, other formations were bearing down on the airfields of Amsterdam-Schipol, Ypenburg and Bergen op Zoom, their object to paralyse Holland's air defences in one blow.

The twenty-seven Heinkels of KG4 swept across Waalhaven and unloaded their bombs with deadly precision. Dozens of troops of the Queen's Regiment were killed when the hangars in which they were billeted collapsed on top of them and caught fire. Thunderous detonations crashed out through the pall of smoke which rose high in the calm air above the aerodrome.

Minutes later, a second formation of German aircraft came in, this time out of the sunrise. They were Junkers 52s, and as they flew over Waalhaven at low altitude the paratroops of the 3rd Battalion, 1st *Fallschirmjäger* Regiment, cascaded from their open doors. Within five minutes the sky was a mass of billowing white canopies as the paras drifted down in a great ring around the airport. One Junkers, hit by flak, swerved violently off course just as its stick of paratroops was leaving it. Helplessly, sucked in by the heated air, they drifted towards the blazing hangars. They were still more than a hundred feet off the ground when their parachute canopies caught fire and they dropped like stones into the inferno. The other paras landed round the airfield perimeter and relentlessly began to close in on the Dutch defences. In the general confusion, six more Ju 52s landed on the airfield; before they had rolled to a stop German troops had spilled from them and were attacking the defenders from the rear. Within twenty minutes it was all over. Hopelessly outnumbered and outfought, the defenders were overwhelmed and the last isolated pockets of resistance mopped up.

Half an hour later, by which time Waalhaven was crowded with Ju 52s, three ungainly Fokker TV bombers of No. 1 Squadron, 1st Air Regiment, lumbered over and dropped a few bombs among the parked transports, one group of which burst into flames. Two of the TVs were quickly shot down by patrolling Me 110 fighters; the third managed to escape.

Waalhaven was in German hands, but the most important objectives still remained to be secured. These were the bridges over the Maas in the centre of the city, and it was essential that the Germans captured them before the Dutch had time to destroy them. To make the invasion's northern flank secure, Holland had to be overrun as quickly as possible. The wide estuaries of the Maas and the Rhine formed a great natural barrier over which there were only three main crossing-points: the bridges at Rotterdam, Moerdijk and Dordrecht. The German airborne forces had to capture these three points in a lightning attack and hold them until the 9th *Panzer* Division fought its way through to them. Once this was achieved, the way into 'Fortress Holland' would be wide open.

The task of securing the bridges was assigned to General Kurt Student's 7th *Fliegerdivision*. Early on 10 May, while *Stukas* attacked defensive positions on the banks of the Maas, 120 paratroops jumped from Ju 52s and captured the Moerdijk and Dordrecht bridges intact. The Dutch counter-attacked furiously at Dordrecht, but the paras managed to hold on.

Meanwhile, at 0700 on the 10th – as the German troops consolidated their positions at Waalhaven – twelve curious aircraft roared along the Nieuwe Maas, six coming from the east and six from the west, converging on Rotterdam. They were obsolete Heinkel He 59 seaplanes, aircraft whose normal task was air-sea rescue. On this occasion, each He 59 carried ten fully-equipped storm troopers. From their base at Bad Zwischenahn, the two flights of seaplanes had followed separate courses so that they would approach Rotterdam from opposite directions, each machine's twin floats almost brushing the surface of the river. Their objective: the bridges over the Maas.

The twelve Heinkels touched down on the water in a flurry of spray and taxied towards the big Willems bridge. The troops scrambled into rubber dinghies and paddled frantically for the river banks. Within minutes they were

8

crouching behind the girders of the twin bridges, heavy machine-guns in position. As the He 59s took off and flew away, their job done, the Dutch launched their first counter-attack. Bullets whined among the girders and chipped splinters of concrete from the bridge walls. The Germans kept up a brisk fire and the Dutchmen fell back, unable to gain a foothold on either bridge. A few minutes later, a tram came rumbling up to the bridges from the south; from it leaped a company of German paratroops fifty strong. They had been dropped a short distance south of the Maas to assist in the capture of the bridges. Dropping under cover beside their comrades, the new arrivals set up their machine-guns, surrounded themselves with belts and clips of ammunition and prepared for a bitter fight. It was to last five days and four nights while a paratroop battalion from Waalhaven tried in vain to battle its way through the streets to reach them. At least they would be safe from air attack; the *Luftwaffe* ruled the sky.

As the sun climbed higher, formations of German bombers, strongly escorted by Messerschmitts, headed west to pound Allied airfields in Holland, Belgium and France. To the aircrews, climbing away on their respective missions, the roads leading through the forests of the Ardennes towards the Meuse presented an almost unbelievable sight. Packed nose to tail, churning slowly forward, was the mightiest concentration of armour in the history of warfare: 1,500 tanks, moving in three great phalanxes. The whole column was a hundred miles long, and behind it, still deep inside Germany, came the infantry divisions whose task it would be to consolidate the ground won by the initial thrust of the *Panzers* – ground over which a path was already being blasted by the bombers.

This was western Europe in May 1940. This was *Blitzkrieg* – Lightning War.

Chapter One

Armstrong was awakened by the sound of the curtains being drawn. He raised himself on one elbow, squinting against the spears of light that entered his room, which faced east, and massaged his forehead.

A figure was silhouetted against the window. The slight stoop of its shoulders as it turned towards him told him that it was his batman, Smithson. Scrawny, with mournful eyes peering past a huge hook of a nose, Smithson didn't look fit to be wearing the uniform of a lavatory attendant, let alone that of an RAF airman; but he was an excellent officer's servant, and he had an uncanny knack of knowing exactly what was going on. On this occasion, however, as the man placed a mug of tea on the bedside locker at Armstrong's elbow, the latter felt that he could well have done without the information Smithson had to impart.

"Mornin', sir," he said, in his nasal cockney accent. "It's five-thirty, sir, and a lovely mornin.' I've run your bath. By the way, sir, the balloon's gone up. Jerry's invaded Belgium and Holland, sir. There's a signal for you, sir. Just come in."

Armstrong sat bolt upright in bed and took the slip of paper from Smithson's hand. He opened it, turning it towards the window so that the early morning light fell on it. It was from the Air Ministry, and addressed personally to Flight Liutenant K. Armstrong, OC Photographic Reconnaissance Flight, RAF Deanland. The handwritten words hit him in the face like a splash of cold water, bringing him wide awake.

"Early indications of enemy airborne landings Belgium/Holland," it read. "Deploy immediately to Berry-au-Bac. Support facilities in place. Confirm."

There was more, but that was the important part. He stuffed the signal into the pocket of his pyjama jacket and, for once, took a swig of the tea that Smithson had brought him. He normally never touched the stuff, which was good for stripping paint, but this time he was glad to feel the impact of the scalding liquid on the back of his throat. It brought him fully alert.

"Where the hell is Berry-au-Bac?" he mused aloud.

"France, sir. About thirty miles from Reims," Smithson told him, as though it were the kind of question he was called upon to answer every day. Armstrong glanced at him as he swung his legs out of bed. "Smithson," he said, "you never cease to astonish me. You'd better pack some kit. There's no telling how long I might be away."

So soon, he thought, as he donned his uniform after a quick bath and shave. It was barely a fortnight since he had got back from Norway, evacuated by the Royal Navy as the Germans closed in on the port of Namsos. Fighting was still going on there, and the two other Spitfires of the PR flight were in northern Scotland, keeping a watch for German warships – in particular for the battlecruisers *Scharnhorst* and *Gneisenau*, which were thought to be operating in the Norwegian Sea.

Within a few minutes Armstrong was on his way to the operations hut, inhaling the fresh Suffolk air as he walked. It was nine months now since he had first arrived at Deanland; then, the place had masqueraded as a civil aerodrome, tenanted by a flying club and manned by personnel dressed in civilian clothes. Those days were gone. The personnel were in uniform, the canvas hangars and wooden huts were camouflaged, there were coils of barbed wire around the perimeter fence, and anti-aircraft machine-gun posts were sited at various points. The airfield was coming alive; he noted with satisfaction that his Spitfire had been pushed from its hangar and was being refuelled. An airman was at work loading the F24 camera into its compartment. Intent on his job, he did not see Armstrong as the pilot walked briskly past.

Armstrong's stomach was rumbling, but breakfast would have to wait. There was much to be done in the meantime. He returned the salute of the armed guard at the door of the operations hut and went inside, his footsteps clattering on the polished linoleum of the corridor that led to the operations room.

Apart from some new maps on the walls, concealed behind roller blinds, the room was exactly the same as it had appeared when he had first walked into it what seemed a lifetime ago, when the world was still at peace. There was one other occupant, an orderly corporal, bending over a teleprinter that had just begun to chatter out a message. He turned and straightened up when he heard Armstrong enter, then returned to his task at the response of a wave from the pilot.

Armstrong passed through a door beside a small briefing dais at the far end of the room. It gave onto another corridor, a short one this time, with a couple of rooms on one side. The door of the first one was open; Armstrong paused at the threshold and looked inside.

A man sat behind a table that was littered with documents. He was old and completely bald. He wore an ancient pinstriped suit topped by a wing collar of the kind affected by the Prime Minister, Neville Chamberlain. But there was nothing ancient about the eyes that greeted the newcomer; they were blue and piercing, the eyes of a young man.

Armstrong came into the room and took off his cap, hanging it on a convenient hook. He nodded at the man behind the desk, who half rose in greeting and then sat down again. The pilot settled himself in a chair opposite before speaking.

"Well, Max. So they are on the move again. How much do you know?"

The man he addressed as Max was something of an enigma. He had been at Deanland when Armstrong first arrived, and the pilot had been firmly advised – warned, more like – against asking questions about Max's background by the previous commanding officer, Wing Commander Horace Royston, who was now a German prisoner of war. What Armstrong did know was that Max seemed to have all the answers, and suspected that he was well up the ladder of Intelligence. Although the old man spoke flawless King's English, several months' association with him had taught Armstrong to detect the undertone of an accent which he only knew to be Lithuanian because Royston had told him.

Max surveyed him, his eyes suddenly hard. He placed his hands on the desk top and pushed himself upright.

"I can tell you what I know better with the help of a map, Kenneth. Shall we go next door?"

Armstrong smiled. Max was the only person he knew, apart from his mother, who addressed him by his full first name. They went into the operations room and Armstrong instructed the orderly corporal to leave them for the time being. Max reached into a pocket of his waistcoat and produced a key, locking the entrance door after the man had passed through. He crossed to one of the concealed maps and pulled a cord; the blind shot up with a rustle and a crack, revealing a relief map of north-west Europe. Max pointed to a green and brown area that covered most of Luxembourg and extended across the frontier into Germany.

"The Ardennes," he said quietly. "First reports are sketchy, but they indicate that the Germans are massing tanks and infantry in this area in readiness to make a thrust towards the river Meuse, here." His finger moved over the map, tracing a line along the blue snake of a river that ran roughly north-south along the western border of Luxembourg until it entered Belgium, where its name changed to the Maas. Armstrong looked closely at it, picking out one name that stood out: Sedan.

13

"If the Germans' intention is to attack here, as seems likely," Max went on, "it will make a mockery of the much-vaunted French main line of defence – the Maginot Line."

Armstrong was familiar with that defensive structure; he had seen its massive fortifications from high altitude, zig-zagging like a brown snake across the landscape, during a reconnaissance flight he had made into Germany soon after his return from Norway. Its origin went back to 1922, when a French Army Commission was appointed to look into the country's existing defence policy and make recommendations for the future. Led by Marshal Joffre, the Commission visited the famous battlefield of Verdun, where a series of underground forts had defied a whole German Army Corps and the biggest concentration of artillery in history for ten months. The French generals were suitably impressed; what might have been the outcome of the war, they thought, and the saving of life and territory, if France had possessed an interlocking web of such forts along the whole of her eastern frontier in 1914!

For the best part of a decade the Commission and successive governments argued over the feasibility of a fortified "eastern wall" running the length of the frontier; one blueprint after another was studied, only to be torn up. On two things only the military were agreed; the fortified front would have to be continuous – and it would cost an enormous sum of money to create. Finally, in January 1930, both chambers of the French National Assembly voted for work on the fortified line to begin immediately and set aside the vast sum of three thousand million francs, to be spread over four years, for its construction. The deadline for its completion was to be 1935, the year in which – under the terms of the Versailles Treaty – French forces of occupation were to be withdrawn from the Rhineland.

The line was to extend from Basle on the Swiss frontier to Longwy, at the junction of the Belgian, Luxembourg and French frontiers. Its strongest points, covering a length of eighty-seven miles, were designed to protect Lower Alsace and the Metz-Nancy sector, both of which were particularly vulnerable to a large-scale attack from the east. The line varied in depth, but at its strongest points it consisted of a series of anti-tank obstacles and barbed wire entanglements facing the frontier, supported by reinforced concrete blockhouses and pillboxes. Behind them was a deep anti-tank ditch, beyond which lay the line's network of underground casemates and forts. Each casemate, protected by up to ten feet of concrete, was equipped with quick-firing anti-tank guns, machine-guns and grenade-throwers; it had a garrison of twenty-five men whose living quarters were on a lower level.

Every three to five miles along the line, supporting the casemates, was a subterranean fort of concrete and steel. These forts were truly remarkable feats of engineering; the biggest, with a garrison of twelve hundred officers and men, consisted of eighteen blockhouses, each with a retractable turret housing guns ranging in calibre from 37-mm to 135-mm. There were powerful generators to supply the forts with heat and light, compressors to ensure a constant supply of fresh air, stores and ammunition magazines, the whole linked by a series of corridors which were completely bombproof and up to a mile and a half long. In the larger forts, a miniature electric railway provided a rapid means of transport for personnel and material. Each fort was divided into two separate units, so that if one was knocked out, the other would continue to function independently, and the field of fire of each fort covered all neighbouring forts and casemates. Backing up the whole structure were mobile infantry units, with supporting artillery, which could be moved up rapidly to support the fort complexes in the event of enemy infiltration.

Work went ahead on the fortifications – known as the Maginot Line after André Maginot, the War Minister of the day – at a fast rate, and its eighty-seven miles of main defences were substantially completed by 1935. By this time the line had already cost seven thousand million francs, far in excess of the budgeted figure, and the cost of maintaining it imposed an almost intolerable burden on a country whose economy was ailing – and one, moreover, where a strong Left Wing, opposed to rearmament in any form, made its voice continually heard. The result, inevitably, was that the French Army was compelled to suffer severe cuts in other areas.

Most serious of all, the Maginot Line remained at best only a partial shield against an attack from the east against metropolitan France. At its northern end there was no extension of the fortifications to cover the 250-mile common frontier between France and Belgium – and this despite the fact that in 1914 the German Army, following the brilliantly-devised Schlieffen Plan, had debouched into France across the drab Belgian plains. There were a number of reasons for this omission, apart from the question of cost. The first, and not the least important, was that an extension of the line would have to pass right through the middle of the big industrial areas around Lille and Valenciennes, which would lead to unacceptable disruption; the second was that Belgium herself, separated from her French ally by a fortified line, might feel justified in adopting a policy of complete neutrality. In view of this, the French were prepared in Belgium's case to adopt an offensive posture – although it went very much against their overall defensive policy – by sending their forces across the border to fight a delaying battle on Belgian soil. This strategy was feasible enough in 1935, when the French Army still enjoyed considerable numerical superiority over the *Wehrmacht*; but by 1939 the German tactics, combining the use of tanks and dive-bombers, had made nonsense of it.

Between 1935 and 1939, then, while the Germans broke all records to develop their offensive capability, the French – like a tortoise retreating into its shell – retired behind the mythical impregnability of the Maginot Line, apparently oblivious to its glaring deficience; deficiencies which should have come to the fore when, in October 1936, King Leopold III of Belgium revoked his country's treaty with France and opted for a return to neutrality. The French northern flank had been wide open ever since.

"And the Germans know it only too well," remarked Max, who had been rapidly filling in the gaps in Armstrong's knowledge of France's defensive system as the two pored over the map in the operations room. "That's why a massive assault in this area is their logical choice. And I will let you into a secret; we have known of their intentions for several months."

Armstrong nodded. "As a matter of fact, I know about that. Wing Commander Royston told me about it. A German communications aircraft, carrying the blueprint for an invasion, strayed over the border last January and the Belgians got hold of the papers. The Belgian High Command wanted the French Army to move up right away, but the move was forbidden by their king. Am I correct?"

Max nodded. "Quite correct. The French will move up now, of course, and so will the British Expeditionary Force, but it will very probably be too late. Plan D, I fear, is doomed before it can be implemented."

Plan D, known also as the Dyle Plan, had its origin in an earlier scheme called the Escaut Plan. Proposed in September 1939 by General Georges, commanding the French North-Eastern Army Zone, it envisaged an advance into Belgium by two armies, one French and one British, to face a German threat and form a defensive line along the Escaut river from the French frontier at Conde as far as Ghent. The plan depended on securing the Belgian Government's approval, and much of it hinged on the ability of the Belgian Army to extend the line and hold it from Ghent to Antwerp. In November 1939, however, Allied intelligence indicated that a German attack would also involve Holland, and since the Escaut Plan did not cover Dutch territory, it was abandoned in favour of a new scheme, Plan D. This envisaged an Allied main line of resistance anchored on the Dyle, which lay further to the east in Belgium and from which a rapid advance could be made into Holland.

In its finalised form, Plan D made provision for the Allied armies to occupy a continuous defensive line from the Dutch border to Mezières, in northern France. In the extreme north, the defence of Holland would rest with eight Dutch divisions; immediately to the south came the French Seventh Army, holding a line between Turnhout and Breda; then the Belgian Army, from Louvain to Antwerp; on the Belgians' right flank the ten divisions of the British Expeditionary Force, lying between Wavre and Louvain and effecting a junction with the French First Army, in position between the BEF and Namur; and finally, between Namur and Mezières on the southern flank of the line, came the French Ninth Army.

"That's the plan," Max explained. "It's a good one, and there is nothing wrong with the fighting troops, although we all know that they lack adequate air support. The main area of concern is not here, in the north, but here, on the Meuse."

His finger moved over the map and traced a rough circle around Sedan.

"The trouble," he continued, "is that the French don't believe the Germans can force a passage through the Ardennes. This sector, therefore, is quite thinly defended by the French Second Army, which has sixteen poorly-equipped and poorly-trained divisions, half of them second class. Their job is to hold a ninety-five-mile stretch of front, and to make matters worse the Maginot fortifications are only half completed here. But ask yourself this: if the Germans don't intend to launch a major attack here, why are they making every effort to shoot down our reconnaissance aircraft?"

"I'd heard that they have been suffering pretty severe losses," Armstrong. "I didn't know that it was particularly bad in that area, though."

"It is," Max remarked grimly. "For some reason the French have been sending their aircraft into enemy territory unescorted, and their reconnaissance squadrons have suffered dreadful losses. That is why they have asked for our help. Our Spitfires are the only reconnaissance aircraft fast enough to make a thorough survey of the area with any hope of survival. Let's go back into my office."

Back in his seat, Max unlocked a desk drawer and withdrew a red folder, which he handed to Armstrong. "Your operational orders," he said. "We have had them for some time; in fact, they were put in place not long after the German invasion plans fell into our hands, and the Joint Air HQ realised that our help would probably be needed. As you will see, they are straightforward enough."

Armstrong flicked through the flimsy pages inside the folder and smiled thinly. "Straightforward, all right," he grunted. "All I have to do is to fly to Berry-au-Bac, top up with fuel, fly at medium level over what is probably the biggest concentration of anti-aircraft guns this side of Berlin, dodge Messerschmitts, and deliver the film to Air HQ. Simple, really."

He handed the folder back to Max. "Well, I suppose I'd better grab a bite of breakfast and get cracking. Oh, there is just one thing."

"What's that?"

"Suppose – just suppose – that the Germans have launched their offensive in France already. Suppose they are halfway to Reims. What then?"

"Come home," Max told him quietly. "By then, it will be much too late."

BATTLE SITUATION: THE ARDENNES, 10 MAY 1940

For the Allied air forces, the enormous mass of men and material that wound its way through the Ardennes on the morning of 10 May represented the target of a lifetime.

But the hours of the morning dragged on, and still no order came to unleash the Allied bombers. In the joint headquarters at Chauny, Air Marshal Arthur Barratt, commanding the British Air Forces in France, and General d'Astier de la Vigerie, commanding the French Northern Zone of Air Operations, paced up and down in frustration as they awaited the necessary signal from the French GHQ. Their anger mounted when, at 0800, they received a signal restricting Allied air operations to fighter and reconnaissance activity. At that very moment the enemy columns, jammed tightly along the narrow roads through the Ardennes, were highly vulnerable to air attack; and yet, because of the French terror of Luftwaffe reprisals and the totally irrational hope of General Maurice Gamelin, the French Commander-in-Chief, that a bombing war might somehow be avoided, the opportunity to hit the invaders hard was being thrown away.

It was not until 1100 that GHQ finally relented – and even then its orders only added to the frustration of the Allied air commanders. They were authorised to attack enemy columns as first priority and *Luftwaffe* airfields as second priority, but built-up areas were to be avoided at all costs. This immediately robbed the first-priority task of much of its effectiveness, since the biggest and most inviting concentrations of enemy armour were to be found in the innumerable hamlets scattered throughout the Ardennes. In addition, the Allied bombers were strictly forbidden to attack enemy industrial areas or centres of communication – an order that directly contravened the operational plans so carefully formulated by the British and French Air Staffs over the previous months. In the end the French day-bomber force, utterly confused by the ambiguity of it all, simply stayed on the ground while General d'Astier begged GHQ for further orders that might clarify the position.

By this time, Air Marshal Barratt's impatience at the apparent lethargy of the French commanders had reached breaking point. Taking the initiative, he telephoned General

Georges, Commander-in-Chief of the forces on the North-Eastern Front, and informed him that he intended to send the light bombers of the RAF's Advanced Air Striking Force, the AASF, into action without delay. Georges murmured, "Thank God!" His men were hard pressed and the *Panzers* were breaking through everywhere. And yet it was Georges himself who had insisted that the Allied air forces should not attack built-up areas.

Most of the AASF's squadrons, based on a number of airfields in Champagne, between Paris and the Meuse, had been at readiness since 0600, with half their available aircraft ready for take-off at thirty minutes' notice and half at two hours' notice. In the few hours since then, however, the German advance had been so rapid that Intelligence had not been able to keep pace with the enemy's movements, and it was not until noon that firm target information was available. A few minutes later, thirty-two Fairey Battle light bombers – one flight each from seven squadrons – took off from their respective bases with orders to attack enemy columns advancing through Luxembourg.

They approached the target in four waves, escorted by a mere eight Hawker Hurricanes, which broke away and patrolled over the city of Luxembourg. The Battles made their attack and encountered no enemy fighters, but they ran into a blizzard of fire from mobile 20-mm cannon and machine-guns and thirteen of them were shot down.

At 1530 the AASF mounted a second attack on the columns of the German Sixteenth Army in Luxembourg, again with thirty-two Battles. This time there was no fighter escort, and a squadron of Messerschmitt 109s came tumbling down on the British bombers. Ten Battles failed to return from this sortie. Twenty-three aircraft out of sixty-four, with as many more so badly damaged as to be out of action for some time, was a fearful rate of attrition, and the AASF flew no more combat sorties that day . . .

Chapter Two

Armstrong found the airfield at Berry-au-Bac without difficulty. It was a grass field, nestling in green, wooded country beside the main road that ran from Reims to Lyon. As he made a gentle descent towards it, hoping that the people down there knew he was coming – his Spitfire, to save weight, was not fitted with a radio – he reflected on his flight from England. The curious thing was that he hadn't seen a single aircraft; he had even begun to wonder whether the rumours of invasion were true.

"Oh, they're true all right," said the duty officer who greeted him as he climbed from the cockpit after taxying to a dispersal point on the southern side of the aerodrome. "The Hurricane squadron based here has been in action since dawn. They've scored some kills, too, and so far they're all OK. They're out now, over Luxembourg. Come and have something to eat while your Spitfire is being refuelled. If I were you I'd be on my way as quickly as possible; Jerry hasn't paid us a visit yet, but I've a feeling he won't be long."

They made the short trip to the mess tent perched on the duty officer's motorbike. Armstrong spotted a number of Fairey Battle light bombers dispersed at the opposite end of the airfield. "Have they been in action yet?" he queried, clinging on grimly as the motor cycle bumped over the grass.

"No," the duty officer shouted back. "The bomber boys are really cheesed off. Their CO keeps ringing up Air HQ every ten minutes, but no luck. If I was them, though, I'd be content to stay on terra firma. Poor buggers," he added. It sounded like an epitaph.

Armstrong found some of the Battle crews drinking tea in the mess tent; they seemed cheerful enough, although they must have known that the odds were stacked against them. Despite himself, because he despised such thoughts, he found himself wondering how many of them would still be around in a couple of days' time.

Armstrong discovered that his companion, a flying officer called Edmonds, was a Hurricane pilot who had been grounded on doctor's orders for a few days because of a chest infection. He brought Armstrong a mug of tea and a plate of bully beef and biscuits. Armstrong wasn't really hungry, but he knew that he would be in a couple of hours' time, so he chewed mechanically on the unappetising fare, conversing with Edmonds between mouthfuls. Edmonds told him that the two AASF Hurricane squadrons had seen a fair amount of action in recent weeks.

"We'd been chasing their reconnaissance aircraft, mostly Dorniers, all through the winter months; knocked down a number of them, too. Then, all of a sudden, they started sending over fighter formations, usually at high altitude. They would try to bounce us as we climbed, making one or two passes and then high-tailing it back into Germany. At first it was just Me 110s we came up against – not much problem with them. But last month we encountered more 109s, and we noticed that the Huns had changed their tactics. Sometimes, two or three squadrons of Messerschmitts would carry out a sweep as far as Metz or Nancy; they would stay up really high and they'd only fight when they had to. Our guess is that they've been experimenting with new battle formations. Oh, and they're not using Dornier 17s as much as they used to; they've been sending over Junkers 88s to do their recces, and they're devilish hard to catch."

Armstrong nodded. "I was on the receiving end of Ju 88s in Norway," he said. "It wasn't pleasant, I can tell you." He gave Edmonds a brief resumé of his reconnaissance activities during the Norwegian campaign, and got the impression that he might as well have been talking about something that happened on the moon. It was understandable; the Hurricane boys in France had been in action almost from the word go, as indeed had their French counterparts.

Changing the subject, he looked around the mess tent. "A bit sparse in here, isn't it?" he commented.

Edmonds grinned. "Oh, we've got a proper mess. It's a chateau at Guignicourt, about four miles away. Very comfortable, too. This is just so the boys can grab a quick snack between sorties. Speaking of which, I think I can hear them coming back. Shall we take a look?"

They went outside into the sunlight. It was late morning and the sun was high; they squinted into it, trying to make out the returning Hurricanes whose Merlin engines they could now hear clearly. Suddenly they were there, three of them, the first to return, slanting down the sky in line astern, well spaced out, engines crackling as the pilots throttled back on the approach to land. There was another sound, too; a shrill whistle as the wind played around the eight gun ports in the wings of each aircraft. That meant the Hurricanes had been in action; if they had not, the little canvas patches glued over the ports to prevent the guns from freezing at altitude would still have been in place.

There were other signs of action, too. The first Hurricane to land had fabric stripped from its rear fuselage. It taxied past the mess tent on its way to the dispersal and the pilot gave Edmonds and Armstrong a thumbs-up sign.

One by one the other Hurricanes came in to land. Armstrong counted twelve – the full squadron. Trucks carrying ground crews followed the aircraft to their dispersals; one of them collected the pilots and brought them to the tent, where they hungrily launched an attack on the food set aside for them. The squadron intelligence officer arrived from somewhere and began to interrogate them as they ate.

"Got a 110," said a tall young pilot officer who was the

pilot of the first Hurricane to land. "Damn' near got me first, though. Cannon shell went right through the fuselage and exploded on the other side. Gave me a hell of a fright. Then he overshot and pow! I had him."

The remark gave Armstrong cause to ponder on the robustness of the Hurricane. If the cannon shell had hit a Spitfire, which had an all-metal fuselage as opposed to the Hurricane's structure of canvas-covered wooden spars, it would most probably have exploded inside and blown the tail off.

Armstrong would have liked to talk to the Hurricane pilots, but he reminded himself that he had a job to do. A refuelling bowser had been parked next to his Spitfire for some time; now, its task completed, it moved off towards the recently-landed Hurricanes.

A corporal on a bicycle came pedalling across the airstrip and, after ascertaining that Armstrong was the Spitfire's pilot, informed him that it was topped up with fuel and ready to fly. Armstrong saw that a couple of ground crew were standing beside the aircraft, having pushed over a trolley-accumulator from one of the Hurricane dispersals. It was time to be off.

Edmonds gave him a lift back across the field and watched as Armstrong climbed onto the Spitfire's wing, having completed the necessary formalities with the ground crew and walked round the aircraft to ensure that everything was in place. The pilot swung his leg over the cockpit side-flap and lowered himself into the seat, the parachute forming a cushion under him. He did up its straps, making sure that they were good and tight, and closed the cockpit flap before fastening the seat harness. He carried out his pre-start checks, gave a signal to the ground crew, then pressed the twin starter buttons. Ahead of him, the propeller gave a few slow turns and then dissolved into a blur as the engine coughed into life in a cloud of blue smoke. One of the airmen unplugged the starter battery, closed the flap on the side of the engine cowling and gave Armstrong the thumbs-up.

The pilot mentally went through his cockpit checks: brakes, trim, flaps, contacts, pressure, petrol and radiator, all OK.

A quick look round, a wave to Edmonds who was sitting astride his motorbike a few yards away. Handbrake off, a touch of throttle and the Spitfire began to roll forward, bumping slowly across the grass, rolling on its narrow-track undercarriage as Armstrong applied coarse left and right rudder alternately, yawing the long nose from side to side to clear the blind spot directly in front of it. He wrinkled his nose; the cockpit reeked of glycol coolant as usual.

He made a final cockpit check as he taxied out and turned into wind, getting a green light from the concrete hut that served as flying control. RAFTS. R for retractable undercarriage, green light on. A for airscrew in fine pitch. F for flaps up. T for trim, just a little aft of centre on the wheel in the cockpit. S for Sperry gyro, caged. Another quick look round; nothing above and behind. He slowly opened the throttle, sending the Spitfire lurching forward across the field. Stick forward to lift the tail, but not too far or the propeller blades would dig into the ground.

The Spitfire bounced two or three times and then became airborne. Armstrong turned, trimmed the aircraft to climb, then held the stick between his knees as he used one hand to pump up the undercarriage, the other resting securely on the throttle lever. The Mk II Spitfire, which was equipping Fighter Command's frontline squadrons, had an automatic undercarriage retraction system, but not so the Mk I, which included his photo-recce PR Mk IB.

With the undercarriage safely retracted, Armstrong settled down for the long climb towards the Belgian frontier, which he planned to cross at 15,000 feet north-east of Montmedy. He then intended to descend, building up speed for a fast seventy-mile run across the Ardennes to Dinant, photographing road junctions where concentrations of enemy vehicles would be likely to show up.

Presently, the broad ribbon of the Meuse crept beneath

the Spitfire's wings. He was scanning the sky constantly now, aware that to anyone flying higher up, his blue-painted aircraft would stick out like a sore thumb against the greens and browns of the landscape. He passed Montmedy and continued on his present course for a while, turning left when he picked up the railway line that ran from Luxembourg to Namur. There seemed to be a lot of smoke rising from the ground away to the right, but he could not see what was causing it.

He forced himself to concentrate on the task in hand, rolling his head constantly to monitor the danger area above and behind, then searching the ground ahead for signs of enemy activity. His first objective was Neufchateau and he map-read his way towards it, taking the Spitfire down in a shallow dive as he approached the ancient town, which was situated on some heights with roads radiating from it in all directions.

Armstrong sped over the town at 5,000 feet, tilting his aircraft in order to obtain a vertical photograph; the camera, mounted in the fuselage side, was designed for oblique photography, and pointed down at an angle of thirteen degrees. No ground fire came up at him, for which he was thankful; he had anticipated being shot at by friendly ground forces as well as by the enemy, for the Spitfire's silhouette was not exactly familiar in these parts.

His relief was short-lived. A few miles further on, about halfway between Neufchateau and Bastogne, intense small-arms fire rose to meet him; he was soon clear of it, but he knew that his aircraft had taken several hits in the wings and fuselage. He could not believe that the enemy had advanced this far already, and could only assume that he had been the target of friendly fire.

As it happened, he was wrong. It was his ill-luck to have flown slap over the top of a German airborne force which had landed at this point in the Belgian Ardennes in the early hours of the morning, just as the gliders were going down on the fortress of Eben Emael. In fact there had been two such operations. In the first, twenty-five Fieseler *Storch* army co-operation aircraft, renowned for their short take-off and landing performance, had deposited 125 volunteers of the German 34th Infantry Division near Esch-sur-Alzette on the Franco-Luxembourg border. The task of the detachment was to hold the crossroards at Esch until General Heinz Guderian's *Panzers* arrived. The *Storchs* made two sorties, and by first light the task force was in position. One of the Germans' first contacts was a bewildered *gendarme*, who politely informed them that they were on neutral territory and asked them to leave. Equally as politely, they arrested him. There were no further incidents before the German ground forces arrived, and by 0900 the forward elements of the 1st *Panzer* Division had reached the Belgian frontier after crossing the whole of Luxembourg with hardly a shot fired.

The more northerly operation ran along similar lines. Here, two assault groups, comprising the 3rd Battalion of the elite *Grossdeutschland* Regiment and a special volunteer force, some 400 men in all, were landed at Nives and Witry, midway between Neufchateau and the towns of Bastogne and Martelange. Their task was to keep the roads to Neufchateau open for the passage of Guderian's tanks, which would then press on towards their main objective: the River Meuse, and the town of Sedan.

The operation, code-named *Niwi*, began at 0420 that morning, when 98 *Storchs* carrying 196 troops took off from Bitburg and Deckendorf and headed for their objectives. Everything did not go entirely as planned. Although the first formation of 56 *Storchs* landed their troops at Witry on schedule, the Nives group of 42 aircraft became badly scattered, and some of the *Storchs* landed as much as nine miles from their objective. It was not until the early afternoon that the two assault groups were able to link up, and it was at precisely this time and place that Armstrong had flown overhead.

A short while later the *Storchs* brought in the second

28

half of the force, which enabled the Germans to beat off attacks by Belgian and French troops until Guderian's armour arrived later that day.

Three or four miles past Witry, Armstrong knew that something was wrong. His oil pressure was rising alarmingly, and it was beginning to feel uncomfortably warm in the cockpit. His instruments told him that his engine was overheating, and he knew that he was going to have to break off the sortie.

He turned back towards the Franco-Belgian border, intent on finding an airfield on the other side. Throttling back as much as he dared, he found that he could just maintain his present altitude. He flew steadily on, smelling his engine growing hotter and hotter all the while, knowing that he was going to have to get down soon or risk the consequences. With an enormous gush of relief he saw the Meuse up ahead, and a few minutes later picked up a town which he identified as Mezières. Searching the area, he found what he was looking for; a light green patch which his trained eyes told him was an airfield.

He judged the wind direction by reference to drifting smoke on the ground and began his approach, operating the undercarriage lever. Nothing happened, except that a red light winked at him mockingly from the instrument panel. Hydraulics shot up, he thought fleetingly. There was no time to worry; only time to act, and act quickly. The oil temperature was nearly off the clock and smoke was trailing from the engine exhaust stubs, growing denser by the second.

He tightened his harness straps and lowered the seat as far as it would go in order to protect his head if the aircraft should flip over on its back. Sliding the hood back, he locked it in position; air rushed into the cockpit and he suddenly realised that he was bathed in a clammy sweat. The smoke from the exhaust stubs was now shot with glowing sparks and glycol fumes were beginning to invade the cockpit.

He was over the airfield boundary now. Vivid details imprinted themselves on his mind; twin-engined aircraft, some intact, some wrecked, dotted here and there among bomb craters. Look for a clear patch ahead. He'd forgotten to do something. Christ! With a hand that was far from steady, he switched off the battered engine and cut off the fuel supply. Far from dying away, the smoke now belching from the exhaust stubs increased in volume.

The grass was a blur beneath the aircraft's wings. Out of the corner of his eye he saw figures running towards him. A glance at the airspeed indicator: ninety miles per hour. Without fully realising it, he had been pulling back gently on the stick, killing the speed. The Spitfire shuddered and he pulled the stick right back, stalling the aircraft.

There was a moment or two of utter silence, followed by an appalling crash as the Spitfire dropped onto the ground, jarring every bone in his body. He had a hazy impression of bits flying off. Fragments of propeller whirled past the cockpit.

He had anticipated the sudden deceleration, but it was far worse than anything he had expected. His seat harness bit deeply into his shoulders as he was hurled violently forward. The world gyrated dizzily as the aircraft slewed round. The port wingtip dug in and then the nose. Suddenly, Armstrong saw nothing but grass and clods of flying earth through the windscreen, and for a terrible moment he thought that the machine really was going to flip over. Then, with a last fearsome crunch and a screech of tearing metal, it flopped back on his belly again.

His first sensation was a numbness in his wrist, and he realised that he had been clutching the now useless control column for dear life.

Letting go, he ripped off his flying helmet and unlocked his harness. Without bothering to unlatch the cockpit door, he heaved himself over the edge, still wearing his parachute, and collapsed onto the buckled and earth-spattered wing. Sliding off, he tottered to his feet and stumbled away from the aircraft, fumbling with the parachute harness's quick-release box as he went. The impediment fell away and he increased his pace, anxious to get well clear, having a good idea of what was about to happen.

The figures were still running towards him. He waved his arms at them frantically.

"Get back!" he yelled, or tried to yell; the words came out as a hoarse croak. "It's going to go up!"

Behind him, there was a dull thud and a roaring noise. He felt a wave of heat on his back and tripped up, sprawling full length on the ground. A man in the dark blue uniform and gold braid of a French Air Force officer bent over him and grasped him under the armpits, pulling him to his feet. Armstrong put a hand on the man's shoulder to steady himself and half-turned to look back at the wreck.

The Spitfire was a mass of flame, spewing a cloud of oily smoke into the air. Somewhere in there, the film he had risked his neck to obtain would be charring away nicely. So, he thought, was his overnight kit, which his batman had stowed in the wing in the space that would normally be occupied by one of the ammunition boxes. He had decided to leave it there in case his return to England should be delayed for any reason.

It would be delayed now, all right.

Armstrong, his legs suddenly weak, sat down heavily on the grass. He spoke passable French, and trawled his brain for an expression that would fit the occasion. He found one word that would do very well.

"*Merde!*" he said, with considerable feeling.

The Frenchman helped him to his feet again and patted him sympathetically on the arm. He introduced himself as Captain Le Roy, and said that he was saddened by Armstrong's predicament. He asked if the Englishman's "Hurricane" had been attacked by enemy fighters. Armstrong pointed out that it was actually a Spitfire, and explained his mission. He also mentioned his belief that he

31

had been damaged by friendly fire, at which Le Roy raised an eyebrow.

"I doubt it, my friend. Our troops and the Belgians have been engaging a force of Germans all day in that very area. Events are overtaking us, you see. The immediate question arises, though, of what we are to do with you. We are in the process of moving to another airfield, and we have no transport to spare to take you to your headquarters at Reims. All I can suggest is that you remain with us for the time being as our guest, so to speak, while we work something out."

And remain with the French Armstrong did, for much longer than he could possibly have envisaged.

BATTLE SITUATION:
THE BRIDGES AT MAASTRICHT, 12 MAY 1940

On 11 May, one low-level attack by eight Fairey Battles was ordered against enemy forces moving up to the Luxembourg border. They never reached the target area; the only crew to return, their aircraft badly hit en route by anti-aircraft fire, reporting seeing several other Battles going down amind heavy flak while still over the Ardennes.

Meanwhile, armour and motorised infantry continued to pour over the Meuse at Maastricht and General Hoeppner's 16th *Panzerkorps*, benefiting from the still-intact bridges over the Albert Canal, thrust on towards Tongeren with strong dive-bomber support. The Belgian Government regarded the destruction of these bridges as vital, and in the small hours of 11 May addressed a desperate plea to the commanders of the Allied air forces to mount attacks on them.

Air Marshal Barratt was the first to respond, and at first light No. 114 Squadron RAF, one of the AASF's two Bristol Blenheim squadrons, was ordered to stand by for the mission. An hour later the Blenheims were fuelled and bombed-up; the crews were briefed and ready to go. Take-off was in fifteen minutes. A light drizzle had fallen shortly before dawn on Conde Vraux airfield – the squadron's base on the north bank of the Aisne not far from Soissons – and the air was fresh and cool as the crews snatched a last cigarette before climbing aboard their aircraft.

Suddenly, nine elongated shapes skipped over a line of trees and fanned out low across the airfield. They were Dornier 17s, and before the startled defences had time to fire a shot the bombers were speeding over the line of parked Blenheims. Showers of 100-pound fragmentation bombs cascaded down and exploded among the British aircraft. The Dorniers turned and came in again, raking the airfield with machine-gun fire. Then, still low down, they disappeared in the direction of the Aisne. Belatedly, a Vickers gun chattered.

The flight line was a shambles. Bodies of airmen sprawled among the shattered wreckage of the Blenheims and columns of oily smoke rose from lakes of burning fuel. In less than a minute, No. 114 Squadron – half the AASF's medium bomber strength – had ceased to exist.

At 1130, the Belgian Air Force itself attempted to destroy the bridges with the most modern bombers it had left: nine British-supplied Fairey Battles, operating from Aeltre airfield. The crews were briefed to attack the bridges at Veldwezelt, Vroenhoven and Briedgen in three flights of three. The mission was a disaster; six Battles were shot down by intense flak before they got anywhere near their targets, and the 100-pound bombs of the three survivors failed to do any damage.

Because of the indecision of the French High Command, it was not until the morning of 11 May that the French day bombers flew their first combat sortie. This was carried out by ten LeO 45s, fast and modern twin-engined bombers, which attacked enemy armour around the bridges at Maastricht. Nine of the bombers returned to base, although all were damaged by the intense flak and several crew members were wounded. The next daylight mission in this sector was flown the next day by eighteen Breguet 693 light assault bombers, escorted by the same number of Morane 406 fighters, which made a gallant attack on enemy columns in the Hasselt-St Trond-Liège-Maastricht area. The Breguet's combat debut had been held up because, even at this late stage, some of the aircraft still lacked bomb-release equipment; it was brought up during the night and hastily installed.

The attack went in at treetop height, the Breguets leap-frogging over obstacles as the roofs of Tongeren rose up in front of the pilots. The main road ahead, flanked by trees and ditches, was jammed with vehicles, rolling towards France and travelling fast.

Strings of glowing shells, thousands of them, reached out towards the speeding aircraft. Flak tore into the leading Breguet; it flicked over on a wingtip, smashed through a row of poplars and exploded in the middle of the road on top of a group of vehicles. A second aircraft, one engine in flames, raced low over the Albert Canal and its pilot made a belly-landing in a French field. He and his crew were among the lucky ones; in all, eight Breguets failed to return from this mission.

The earlier annihilation of the AASF's two Blenheim squadrons meant that the vulnerable Battle units would once again have to be sent into action in daylight, even though Air Marshal Barratt was well aware that such a course would be little short of suicide. Barratt had little choice; he was under continual pressure from the French and some sort of air effort had to be made, even though it would almost certainly result in the loss of a high percentage of the AASF's crews. Nevertheless, he stressed that an attack on the bridges at Maastricht by the Battles was to be strictly a job for volunteers.

One hundred and twenty miles from Maastricht, not far from Reims, lay the little grass airfield of Amifontaine, the base of No. 12 Squadron. A little after 0800 on this beautiful

Whit Sunday morning, the squadron's crews – thirty young men in all – were crammed into the small operations hut listening in silence as the deputy CO, Squadron Leader Lowe, told them that he was calling for six volunteer crews to attack the bridges at Vroenhoven and Weldwezelt. With the whole squadron clamouring to be given a chance, Lowe finally settled for the six crews already on standby. Three Battles would attack the bridge at Weldwezelt, and three the bridge at Vroenhoven. The former was to be the objective of 'B' Flight, led by twenty-one-year-old Flying Officer Donald Garland, whose nickname, predictably, was 'Judy'. Garland's opposite number of 'A' Flight was Flying Officer Norman Thomas, who would lead the attack on the Vroenhoven bridge.

Thomas was the first to take off, followed by Pilot Officer Davy. The third member of 'A' Flight, Pilot Officer Brereton, had mechanical trouble with his aircraft and had to be left behind. Five minutes later, Garland's Battle was also airborne, followed by the two machines piloted by Flying Officer McIntosh and Sergeant Fred Marland. Thomas and Davy climbed steadily at 160 mph, levelling off at 7,000 feet. Scattered cloud was creeping across the sky from the east. Thomas glanced at his watch: it was 0900. Tongeren was dead ahead. At that moment a heavy flak barrage erupted around the Battles. It came as a nasty surprise; there had been no indication that the Germans had advanced so far. Thomas and Davy came down to 5,000 feet and altered course north-east, heading straight for the target.

Five minutes ahead of the Battles, the eight Hurricanes of No. 1 Squadron were also heading for Maastricht. Two more Hurricane squadrons, Nos. 85 and 87 of the British Expeditionary Force's Air Component, had also been detailed to provide fighter cover, but No. 1 was first on the scene. High over the Albert Canal, the fighter pilots caught sight of a swarm of glittering crosses. They were the Messerschmitt 109s of *Jagdgeschwaders* 21 and 27 – almost a hundred fighters.

Without hesitating, No. 1 Squadron's CO, Squadron Leader 'Bull' Halahan, gave the order to attack. In the brief dogfight that followed, the squadron shot down three Me 109s and lost two of its own aircraft, one pilot being captured and the other – Halahan – eventually returning to base after making a forced landing in Belgium.

Under cover of the diversion, Thomas roared over the Maastricht-Tongeren road towards his objective, the concrete bridge at Vroenhoven. An Me 109 appeared off to starboard and began to close in, but Thomas held his course. Then the enemy fighter turned and went after Davy, who sheered off into a cloud. The flak was coming up thick and fast now. Thomas pointed the Battle's nose at the bridge ahead and eased forward the control column. The altimeter unwound rapidly and at 3,000 feet Thomas pressed the bomb release. One of his 250-pounders dropped away, followed by the other three, singly. The Battle came out of its dive and raced across the canal at less than 100 feet, hit again and again by shells. Thomas skipped over a German convoy, then the engine died and he brought the aircraft down for a belly-landing. Dazed but unhurt, the crew scrambled out of the wreck and were taken prisoner.

Diving behind his leader, having managed to shake off the Me 109, Pilot Officer Davy saw Thomas's bombs erupt on the far end of the bridge. He dropped his own bombs from 2,000 feet and, to his disappointment, saw them explode in the water and on the canal bank. He turned away and raced for safety, chased by the flak, and at that moment he was attacked by another Me 109. His rear-gunner damaged the fighter and drove it off, but not before cannon shells had set fire to the Battle's port fuel tank. Davy ordered his crew to bail out, and was about to follow them over the side when the fire suddenly went out. He nursed the crippled aircraft towards base, and was only a few miles from home when he ran out of fuel and had to come down in a field. A few hours later Mansell, Davy's observer, arrived back at Amifontaine, but Patterson, the gunner, had not been so lucky. He came down behind the German advance and was captured.

The bridge at Vroenhoven still stood. Five minutes after Thomas's attack, Garland's flight was approaching its metal twin at Veldwezelt. Garland favoured a low-level attack, and the three Battles swept across the Belgian landscape at fifty feet. In line astern they plunged into the writhing cloud of flak bursts. Flying Officer McIntosh's aircraft was hit almost immediately and burst into flames; despite severe burns, the pilot managed to jettison his bombs and made a perfect belly landing on the far side of the canal. The crew got clear and were taken prisoner.

A Battle staggered out of the smoke, burning from wingtip to wingtip. It was Sergeant Marland's aircraft. It went into a steep climb, then flicked over and dived vertically into the ground. There were no survivors. The third Battle – Garland's – suddenly appeared over the bridge, turning steeply, shedding fragments as the flak hit it. Leaving a thin trail of smoke, it dived into the western end of the bridge and there was a terrific explosion as its bombs exploded.

The blast severely damaged the bridge, but within minutes German sappers were erecting pontoons alongside it and there was hardly more than thirty minutes' delay in the flow of traffic across the canal.

A month later, Garland and his observer, Sergeant Tom Gray, were each posthumously awarded the Victoria Cross. In one of those odd injustices of war, their gunner, Leading Aircraftman Reynolds, received nothing more than a posthumous promotion to the rank of corporal.

This was Belgium in May 1940. This was courage and self-sacrifice over and above the call of duty. And it was only the beginning.

Chapter Three

Armstrong had been terrified on numerous occasions since he had first tasted combat, but he had to admit to himself that the flight from Mezières to the French reconnaissance squadron's new base at Martigny, in Lorraine, was probably the most frightening experience of his life.

While the French prepared to evacuate Mezières, Captain Le Roy had worked a minor miracle and had managed to establish telephone contact with Joint Air HQ at Chauny, so that the RAF pilot had been able to pass on the information that he was safe and well, if somewhat shaken. He had also given a progress report, based on his own recent observation, on the extent of the German advance into Belgium. Then he had explained his predicament, and asked for confirmation that he was to remain with the French for the time being, until he could join up with some RAF unit and make his way back to England. The authorisation was readily forthcoming, and Armstrong suddenly found himself in the semi-official role of RAF liaison officer with the French Air Force's 33rd Reconnaissance Group.

While the aircrews flew out in their surviving aircraft, the ground crews travelled by road and an ancient Potez 54 bomber-reconnaissance aircraft arrived to evacuate the handful of pilots, gunners and observers whose aircraft had been destroyed on the ground by enemy air attack. Armstrong had counted himself lucky to be assigned a place on this machine, an opinion that had changed very quickly once it had got airborne.

The distance from Mezières to the new airfield, which

lay a few miles to the south-west of Nancy, was just over a hundred miles. It was clear from the outset what was going through the mind of the French pilot, a sallow, grey-haired individual who was not given to smiling a great deal; if there was a danger of being attacked by enemy fighters, he wanted to be certain of getting down as quickly as possible – which meant flying the whole trip at a hundred feet or less.

The Potez, a high-wing aircraft with twin engines slung underneath on struts, chugged along at 120 miles per hour or thereabouts, leap-frogging woods and villages and wallowing dangerously in ground turbulence. It reeked of aviation fuel, a fact that was totally ignored by the half-dozen French airmen who shared the draughty cabin with Armstrong; they chain-smoked pungent *Caporal* cigarettes as though each one was to be the last, which they probably thought it would be.

Armstrong had stripped off his flying overall and had rolled it up to sit on, there being no seats in the Potez's fuselage. His companions glanced at his RAF tunic and wings curiously and he had the impression that they would have liked to talk, but the interior of the aircraft was so noisy that speech was impossible. A few minutes into the flight one of them produced a bottle of cognac and passed it round, inviting Armstrong to take a swig. The fiery liquor produced a sense of well-being that vanished abruptly when the pilot stood the Potez on a wingtip to avoid some obstacle which he had spotted at the last moment. The aircraft returned to level flight, creaking and groaning alarmingly, and the bottle went round again speedily.

At last, after what seemed an age, the pilot slammed the Potez onto the ground at its destination and, without stopping the engines, appeared from the cockpit and brusquely told everyone to get out as quickly as they could. They did so thankfully, feeling more than a little shaky. A miniature storm of cut grass whirled around them as the Potez pilot gunned his engines and taxied away to turn into the breeze. They watched briefly as the ungainly machine lumbered off and flew away in the direction it had come, still dodging the treetops. What the RAF would term 'hedge-hopping', Armstrong discovered later, the French called '*rase-motte*', which translated as 'clod-shaving'.

The small group made its way towards the aerodrome buildings, some wooden huts on the perimeter of the field. Martigny airfield, Armstrong saw, was situated on a plateau and was completely surrounded by woods in which clearings had been cut as dispersal areas. The Potez 63s had already arrived and had been pushed into the shelter of the trees. The natural camouflage was excellent and the place would be very difficult to spot from the air, which probably accounted for the fact that it had not yet been bombed. The village of Martigny-les-Gerbonvaux was a mere half-mile away, and Armstrong discovered that the personnel were billeted there.

Captain Le Roy emerged from one of the huts to meet the new arrivals. Grinning, he shook Armstrong by the hand.

"So," he said, "you survived the experience?"

Armstrong knew exactly what he meant. "Only just," he admitted. "I wonder where that fellow learned to fly?"

Le Roy laughed. "In Africa, I understand. He is well known to us, and something of a character. Before the war he was a pilot with the postal service on the West African route. He has sand in his boots, like the *Légionnaires*. Knows more about the Sahara than anyone I have ever met. He is, as you have no doubt noticed, *très sérieux*, but I expect that is a consequence of several years spent in the anticipation of having his balls removed by the Tuareg. Yet even our blue-veiled nomad friends have their price; several airmen who have made forced landings in the Sahara have been returned intact, after the appropriate ransom was paid. Others, unfortunately, were not." He shrugged philosophically.

Armstrong noticed that, in addition to the Potez reconnaissance aircraft, several squat, radial-engined fighters were parked among the trees. He could not identify them, and asked Le Roy what they were. The other informed him that they were American-built Curtiss Hawks, with which several French fighter groups were equipped. A flight of them had been deployed to Martigny to provide escort for the Potez 63s and also for air defence.

"I was an Air Force test pilot when the first Hawks were delivered in the spring of 1939," he explained, "and had the opportunity to fly them on several occasions. They are robust, but they suffer from a poor armament of only four machine-guns, which freeze up easily, and they do not have self-sealing fuel tanks, which makes them vulnerable in combat. But it is a nice aircraft to fly, and is very manoeuvrable, with a particularly fast rate of roll – faster, even, than that of your Spitfire, which I have also flown." He grinned and tapped the side of his nose with his index finger.

Armstrong expressed his surprise, and the Frenchman explained that he had been one of two test pilots sent to England to fly the Spitfire in September 1938. "We wanted a hundred of them by September 1939," he said, "but your government said that they could not fulfill such an order, because all the Spitfire production was allocated to the RAF. The American Curtiss Company, on the other hand, told us that they could deliver the Hawk – and, since our own new single-seat fighters would not be ready for some time, we had to be content with that. It is a pity." He shook his head sadly.

The sun was setting in a sky that was almost cloudless. Armstrong asked Le Roy if there would be any flying that night, and the Frenchman told him that two aircraft were to make reconnaissance sorties of the Saarbrucken sector. "For myself, I shall not be flying again until tomorrow," he said. "In the meantime, I intend to enjoy a glass of wine and some good food in the village *auberge*, where I trust you will join me. I have been allocated a room there, and I expect the innkeeper will be able to fit you in, too." He looked Armstrong up and down and smiled. "No doubt you will wish to refresh yourself. I shall acquire some soap, a razor and a towel for you. Your socks, I regret, you will have to wash yourself."

Armstrong laughed; he was already developing a deep liking for the French pilot, whose sense of humour seemed to be in much the same mould as his own. Collecting a couple of fellow pilots, whose names Armstrong immediately forgot, they set off down the slope towards the village, following a path that wound its way between the trees. On reaching the main street, Armstrong noticed that many houses had a steaming muckheap piled in front of them, and commented on this to his companions. They laughed as though he had made a huge joke.

"In Lorraine, it is a sign of prosperity," Le Roy explained, still chuckling. "They are strange people; a little cold, you might think on first meeting them. No, that is not the right word; they are reserved, as you English would say. You will doubtless feel at home here." The Frenchmen laughed again, good-naturedly, and Armstrong was suddenly struck by their apparent lack of concern that their world was in the process of falling apart round their ears. My God, he thought with some alarm, they really believe that they are going to beat the Germans, and that this war is going to be over in just a few weeks. Hasn't anyone told them that their Maginot Line is worse than useless, and that the Germans are pouring round the end of it?

He made an effort to shrug off his sudden melancholy as they reached the inn. The door was open and they trooped inside, Le Roy leading the way. The entrance gave access to a surprisingly large room, lit by the last rays of the sun. A few French officers and some locals were already seated at well-scrubbed, white-topped tables, sipping wine.

At the far side of the room there as a long counter, with bottles of wine arranged on it like guardsmen on parade. Le Roy made straight for it and rapped on it with his knuckles. After a few moments an elderly man with an enormous white moustache emerged from a side room, clutching a grubby cloth. He surveyed the newcomers without smiling, contenting himself with raising an eyebrow. Le Roy nodded affably at him and informed him that he was given to understand that rooms had been allocated.

The innkeeper peered at him with watery eyes. "Two rooms, to be exact, *monsieur*. I regret that you will have to share."

Le Roy spread his hands. "*Diable!* Well, I suppose that it is war, and we must make the best of it. My friend here, incidentally, will require a razor and some soap, if that is possible, for he lost his belongings when the *Boche* shot down his aircraft."

"It is possible, *monsieur*." He smiled unexpectedly and extended a hand towards Armstrong, his gaze taking in the pilot's blue-grey uniform. "I take you for an Englishman," he said. "You are welcome here. I fought alongside the English, on the Somme. I am Raymond Bessodes. We should have destroyed these pigs utterly, in nineteen-eighteen. Do you not agree?"

Armstrong thought it prudent to agree wholeheartedly, since he was famished and would have killed for a drink.

The innkeeper stuck his head round the jamb of a door that led to a room in the rear of the building and called out to someone. A minute later a tall woman emerged, dressed all in black and with her hair tied back in a severe bun. Madame Bessodes had a face like a hatchet, which doubtless accounted for her husband's miserable expression. She carried a rough towel and a bar of soap which she handed to the pilot on Bessodes' instructions, muttering something to the effect that he would have to find a razor for himself, and turned on her heel.

Bessodes shrugged and gave Armstrong a look that spoke volumes, then beckoned to the pilot to follow him up a winding staircase to the room which, he learned, he was to share with Le Roy. There were three beds, or rather cots, in it, all neatly made up. Armstrong dropped his rolled-up flying overall on one and thanked the inkeeper for his hospitality, telling him that he would be back downstairs directly; Bessodes nodded and made himself scarce after pointing out a washstand with a large bowl of water on it.

Armstrong took his forage cap from the pocket of his tunic, where he had stowed it before take-off from Berry-au-Bac that morning (was it only that morning? he asked himself, with a sudden shock) and hung it on a peg behind the door. Then he stripped off to the waist and sluiced himself down thoroughly. The water was cold, but he welcomed that, for it was refreshingly pleasant on his hot and sticky body.

Half an hour later he was back with the others, sitting at one of the scrubbed tables and tucking into a huge bowl of heavily-seasoned stew whose main ingredient, he discovered, was goat. Taken with chunks of white bread and washed down with red wine, he found it delicious. Between mouthfuls, he conversed with his companions as best he could, although they were several glasses of wine ahead of him and he found their boisterous *argot* – slang – difficult to understand. They didn't seem to have a care in the world; it was though tomorrow didn't exist.

Suddenly, to his surprise, he found that he was being shaken out of a doze by Le Roy. The Frenchman grinned at him. "Too much of Lorraine's good wine, my friend?"

Armstrong shook his head and looked around. The lights were on in the room and someone had drawn the curtains. He felt dog-tired, and although the food and wine had certainly helped to induce his weariness, they were not the primary cause. He was aware that he was suffering from reaction, the delayed effects of his crash-landing. He was conscious that he ached all over.

It was a condition that a good sleep would cure. He

excused himself and made his way upstairs to the bedroom. The curtains were open and there was just enough light to see that a candle had been placed on the bedside table, with a box of matches next to it. He closed the curtains and lit the candle, then stripped off his uniform, hanging it behind the door. His shirt and underwear he left in a small heap beside the bed. Absent-mindedly, he noticed that the water bowl had been refilled. Madame Bessodes, he told himself, was no oil painting, but she was certainly efficient.

He climbed between the sheets and prepared to blow out the candle, then decided to leave it lit so that Le Roy could find his way around the room without tripping over anything. An instant later, as though someone had turned a switch, he was asleep.

Armstrong slept the sleep of the drugged. He did not hear Le Roy come in, nor did he hear the Frenchman leave again, early the next morning. The curtains were still closed when he awoke, but their thickness could not conceal the fact that it was broad daylight outside.

He got out of bed and opened the curtains, then looked at his watch; it was seven-thirty. He struggled for a moment to remember what day it was, then realised that it must be Saturday. Saturday, the eleventh of May. Turning back to the interior of the bedroom, he saw to his surprise and delight that his shirt and underclothing had been laundered and had been arranged in a neat pile on top of a chest of drawers. His uniform, too, had been brushed and pressed and was on a hanger behind the door. Madame Bessodes, he told himself, must have been up and about until the small hours. There was also a razor, placed next to his laundry. He fingered his chin, feeling the rough stubble, and decided that a shave was going to be his first priority, but the washing bowl was missing. He was wondering what to do about that when there was a rap on the door.

Realising that he was stark naked, he hurriedly dived back into bed before calling *"Entrez!"* A moment later

45

Madame Bessodes came in, bearing the missing bowl; it had steam rising from it. She bade him good morning as she placed the bowl on the washstand, and asked him if he had slept well. He told her that he had, and tried to thank her for washing his clothing. She waved his thanks aside and, fishing in her apron pocket, produced a note which she handed to him, explaining that it was from Captain Le Roy. "I will provide breakfast for you in twenty minutes, *monsieur*," she told Armstrong, in a tone that suggested she would brook no excuse for lateness.

Armstrong read the note, which was an instruction to make himself known to the *adjutant* – the rank corresponded roughly with the RAF's warrant officer – who was in charge of running the airfield's administration. There was, the note stressed, no hurry at all to report in. Nevertheless, Armstrong shaved quickly and then washed himself from head to foot; it wasn't as good as a bath, but it was better than nothing at all. He allowed himself the luxury of soaking his feet in the bowl for a few moments, then dried himself off and got dressed.

There was no sign of the innkeeper downstairs, but Madame Bessodes made the pilot sit down at one of the tables and, to his astonishment, brought him a plateful of eggs and cold slices of ham, along with a bowl of very milky tea. "*Voilà*," she said, "*le petit déjeuner anglais pour vous.*" It was not exactly an English breakfast, as she claimed, but he realised that she had made a considerable effort to please him and he expressed his gratitude as best he could. To his even greater amazement, she smiled at him and patted him lightly on the shoulder before disappearing into the kitchen.

A few moments later she returned, carrying a framed photograph which she showed to him hesitantly. A round-faced young man in French naval uniform stared out at him. "My son," she explained. "He will be about the same age as you . . . He is in the Mediterranean and safe from the war, I pray. He serves on a great battleship, the *Bretagne*, at a place called Mers-el-Kebir. Better for him to be there than here, I think."

Armstrong murmured something and handed the photograph back to her. She gave a sigh, and returned to her chores. Strange, the pilot thought, how war and danger compels people to confide details of their private affairs to total strangers . . . the little things that are their pride.

He finished his breakfast and carried the utensils into the kitchen, placing them on a table. Madame Bessodes was busying herself at the sink, her back to him, and he sensed that she was crying. So as not to embarrass her, he left without a word.

The morning was bright and clear and filled with birdsong, and Armstrong found himself whistling as he made his way through the woods towards the airfield. Two sentries challenged him as he reached the gate, and although he had left his identity documents in England – a standard procedure before flying on operations, as each aircrew member had his identity disc around his neck by way of identification – the guards were satisfied by Le Roy's note and one of them escorted Armstrong to the *adjutant*'s office in one of the wooden buildings.

The *adjutant*, a much-decorated veteran of the last war, greeted Armstrong affably enough and gave him some coffee, but seemed at a loss when it came to finding the RAF pilot something to do. All the reconnaissance aircraft and their escorting fighters – except one, which had been undergoing repair – were airborne, and it would be some time before they returned. Then the *adjutant* had a brainwave; would the RAF *capitaine* care to inspect the Curtiss Hawk that was still on the ground? The mechanics, he assured Armstrong, would be happy to show him the cockpit.

He led the pilot out to the aircraft, which stood in a clearing facing outwards on to the airstrip. The repairs to the engine had been completed and the mechanics were about to run-up the motor to see if everything worked.

47

The Hawk, Armstrong found, was already armed and almost fully fuelled; its pilot had already taken off on a mission the previous day when engine trouble had forced him to turn back. This morning, in another aircraft, he was somewhere over the Maginot Line.

Armstrong stood on the Hawk's wing and peered into the cockpit as the mechanic who was already sitting inside, ready to start the big Pratt and Whitney Twin Wasp radial engine, showed him where all the switches were. The cockpit, Armstrong noted, wasn't much different from that of a Spitfire or Hurricane, except that it was roomier and the guns – two .50 and two .30 calibre weapons – were fired by triggers rather than a button. The flap and undercarriage levers, he saw, were a little too close together for comfort; it would be very easy to mistake one for the other.

The mechanic signalled that he was going to start the motor. Armstrong nodded and jumped down off the wing, wandering out of the trees into the sunlight. Behind him, the engine gave a couple of bangs and then burst into life, emitting a cloud of blue smoke. It roared throatily for a minute as the mechanic opened the throttle to clear excess oil from the plugs, then the noise died away to a steady rumble as the man brought the throttle setting to 'idle' while he checked the engine instruments.

A shadow rippled over the grass of the airstrip. Armstrong looked round, peering into the eastern sky, squinting into the sun which was now high above the treetops. A moment later, a twin-engined aircraft roared low over the aerodrome, the sound bringing personnel tumbling out of the buildings. There were black crosses under the aircraft's wings; it was a Dornier 17.

Something fell from the Dornier's belly and hit the ground right in the centre of the airfield. There was a thud and a cloud of bright yellow smoke burst from the object, billowing upwards in the still air. Still keeping low, the Dornier sped away from the field, pursued by some ineffectual bursts of machine-gun fire. Armstrong saw it turn steeply in the distance, coming round in a circle that would keep it well clear of any defensive fire, but at the same time enable its crew to keep the smoke marker in sight and guide the bombers that must be following directly on to it.

Armstrong did not pause to think. Turning on his heel, he dashed back into the clearing, thrusting aside the startled ground crew and leaping onto the wing of the Hawk. The man in the cockpit, who had heard nothing above the noise of the engine, looked at Armstrong as though he had gone mad.

"*Vite, vite!*" the RAF pilot yelled at him, pointing at the sky. "Get out, quick! The Germans are here!"

Suddenly white-faced, the man scrambled from the cockpit and dropped from the wing onto the ground. Armstrong looked inside for a second; there was no parachute, just a cushion of some sort which the mechanic had placed in the seat pan where the parachute normally fitted. There was no time to worry about that now.

Settling himself into the cockpit, he strapped himself in quickly, fumbling with the unfamiliar harness. He released the brakes and, holding the stick back, opened the throttle slowly. The Hawk began to move, its speed inceasing, and left the shelter of the trees. A figure came running towards it, gesticulating wildly, and Armstrong recognised the *adjutant*. The pilot took no notice of him and taxied on, opening the throttle wider. As the speed built up he relaxed the backward pressure on the stick, allowing the tail to lift off the ground. He now had a clear view ahead past the big radial engine.

Armstrong risked a glance back over his shoulder; as yet, there was no sign of the incoming bombers. He opened the throttle to its fullest extent and the Hawk gathered speed, bouncing across the grass past the yellow smoke marker. With no wind to shorten its take-off run, the aircraft remained firmly glued to the ground. The airfield boundary was looming up ahead of it. With the throttle hard up against the stops, Armstrong seized the flap lever and pulled it. The big flaps went down and the Hawk suddenly bounded into the air. With relief, Armstrong saw the airspeed beginning to build up. He pulled up the flaps and raised the undercarriage, hauling the fighter round in a steep climbing turn. The cockpit canopy was still open and he decided to leave it that way for the time being, so as to provide an unobstructed all-round view.

Armstrong brought the aircraft round through 180 degrees, still climbing, and wished that he was in a Spitfire; the Hawk climbed like a brick, the altimeter needle, calibrated in metres, creeping round the dial with painful slowness. Squinting into the sun, he saw the enemy bombers; they were Dorniers, like the one that had dropped the marker, and he counted six of them, flying in two tight 'vics' of three, one behind the other. They were flying at about 3,000, half a mile from the airfield.

Armstrong levelled out at the Dorniers' altitude and went head-on for the middle bomber in the first flight. The Curtiss was fitted with an old ring-and-bead gunsight and the bomber grew larger in it with frightening speed. Armstrong unconsciously crouched lower in the cockpit, making himself as inconspicuous as possible, and squeezed both triggers on the control column.

The Hawk shuddered as all four machine-guns opened up and the rapidly expanding silhouette of the Dornier trembled in the windscreen. Grey smoke trails speared out towards it, converging on it. In the bomber's glasshouse nose, a light twinkled; the German gunner was returning fire. Then the nose fragmented and shattered as Armstrong's bullets found their mark.

There was no time to see the end result of his shooting. A collision was a hair's breadth away. Pulling back frantically on the stick, he leapfrogged over the German aircraft, catching a glimpse of its upper-surface camouflage: angular patches of dark and light green, forming a pattern like splinters of broken glass.

Then he was bearing down on the second flight of Dorniers, guns hammering again as he repeated his attack. The leading bomber pulled up suddenly in a climb, exposing its pale blue belly. Its companions on either side broke away sharply to left and right and Armstrong saw his bullets hit the Dornier's underside in a series of sparkling flashes. Then the sky ahead of him was filled with a great fiery balloon of red and black, surrounded by whirling debris, as the Dornier's bomb load exploded.

He shut his eyes and flew straight into the inferno. There was a moment's consciousness of searing heat and of choking, oily fumes mingled with the acrid smell of explosives. Something struck his aircraft with a thud. Then he was through into clear sky, coughing violently.

He opened his eyes and looked outside. The first thing he saw was a dark, sticky mass, glued to his left wing root by the airflow. It took him seconds before he realised that he was looking at a man's entrails.

Armstrong's stomach rose into his mouth and he stuck his head out of the other side of the cockpit. Madame Bessodes' egg breakfast whirled away in the slipstream. Shaking violently, Armstrong risked another look; the glutinous mass was still there. He remembered reading an account of the battle of Trafalgar, when sailors on Nelson's flagship, the *Victory*, had used shovels to prise the remains of men off the bulwarks . . .

Still trembling, he forced himself to concentrate on the job in hand and turned, heading back towards the airfield. Smoke was rising from it, and from clumps of debris that lay in a field just short of it, the remnants of the Dornier he had destroyed.

There was no sign of the other bombers. Armstrong looked behind him to make sure that there was nothing sinister on his tail, then throttled back and began his descent towards the aerodrome. Lowering his undercarriage and flaps, he looked ahead and saw to his surprise that the smoke was coming from a crashed aircraft, its tail sticking out from a clump of trees some distance away. From its twin fins he identified it as one of the Dorniers, presumably the first one he had fired at.

He landed safely between a scattering of fresh bomb craters and taxied in, coming to a stop close to his original dispersal. Wearily, still feeling queasy, he switched off the engine and climbed unsteadily from the cockpit, carefully keeping to the starboard side to avoid the mess on the port wing.

He was only half aware of the ground crew clustering around him, congratulating him. Someone thrust a bottle of cognac into his hand and he raised it to his lips, drinking deeply, washing the bile from his throat.

A few minutes later, the reconnaissance squadron and its fighter escort returned from its mission over enemy territory. Two of the Potez 63s were missing. One of them was Le Roy's.

BATTLE SITUATION,
13 MAY 1940: THE MEUSE

The German assault troops had been moving down through the woods towards the river crossing points throughout the early hours of the morning. Most of the soldiers were red-eyed through lack of sleep, exhausted after their long forced marches through the Ardennes and soaked through by the dripping vegetation of the forest, for it had rained heavily during the night. Nevertheless, there was to be no respite for them; the momentum of the German assault could not be allowed to falter.

During the morning of the 13th, which dawned bright and sunny with a few tendrils of mist drifting over the Meuse and the woods on either side, the heavy artillery of the French X and XVIII Corps opened up on the river crossing points, strategic road junctions and the approaches to the Meuse. The bombardment lasted until midday, and then the French began to run out of ammunition. Apart from the general confusion that prevailed, fresh supplies coming up from the rear were subjected to incessant air attacks by the *Luftwaffe*. Requests for further supplies of ammunition sent through urgently to HQ Second Army never arrived, or if they did they were ignored.

Up until noon, the *Luftwaffe* attacked the French defences on the Meuse in relatively small numbers, the forward positions being hit by groups of half a dozen *Stukas* or medium bombers. Then, in the afternoon, the full weight of two *Fliegerkorps* was hurled against the real pivot of the battle, in support of the armoured thrust at Sedan. *Luftwaffe* orders were to pin down the French defences while German ground forces established a bridgehead.

The first phase of the assault unfolded on schedule at 1600, with a highly effective precision attack by *Stukas* on French artillery positions on the west bank of the Meuse. This was followed within minutes by a second raid, this time by Dornier 17s – and so it went on for hours on end, with successive waves of bombers droning over the river, unloading their sticks with deadly accuracy, and turning for home in almost leisurely manner. French fighters tore gaps in their ranks, but more often than not, the Messerschmitts prevented the French fighter groups from coming anywhere near the bomber formations.

For the defending French troops, the air attacks were a nightmare. Most of their air-raid shelters were only half completed and afforded hardly any protection from the onslaught. Even before the air attack was over, four brigades of German 105-mm guns opened up a heavy fire on the French X Corps sector. Under cover of the bombardment, the German infantry launched themselves across the Meuse on river boats and rafts, sheltered to some extent by the vast cloud of dust and smoke that swirled across the river from the bombing on the opposite bank.

Dazed and bewildered, the French defenders began to emerge from their shelters to be confronted by the first waves of German shock troops, storming up the river bank towards them. One by one, the French positions collapsed under the relentless pressure, many of them being taken from the rear by the speed of the German thrust. Shortly after 1800, ten batteries of X Corps artillery fell intact into German hands. They had been abandoned by their crews as soon as German troops approached to within half a mile. While 1st *Panzer*'s assault troops and the *Grossdeutschland* Regiment crossed to the west of Sedan, 10th *Panzer*'s assault group stormed the river banks at Wadelincourt, to the south-east of the town. Progress was slow here, for the air attacks and shelling had not suceeded in destroying many of the defensive bunkers, and these put up heavy machine-gun fire against the attackers.

The main problem for the Germans here was the lack of artillery support, and flanking fire from the Maginot Line fortifications was giving them trouble. There were delays, too, in the assault of the 2nd *Panzer* Division, which was to have stormed the Meuse at Donchery to the west of Sedan. In fact, only the advance elements of 2nd *Panzer*, the reconnaissance battalion and the motorcycle battalion, together with the division's heavy artillery, saw action on 13 May, and these did not succeed in forcing a crossing. Most of the division's tanks were still on the Samois river, and would not arrive until after dark. These setbacks, however, were more than compensated for by the rapid thrust of the 1st *Panzer* Division. By nightfall, the German assault troops had torn their way through the French defences in the Marfee Wood region, two miles inland from Sedan. By midnight the division's rifle brigade was pushing still deeper into French territory, while a battalion of the *Grossdeutschland* Regiment mopped up around Wadelincourt.

At Gaulier, German engineers built a bridge across the river, enabling the 2nd *Panzer* Division to begin moving across at dawn, the tanks rolling past thousands of French prisoners herded into pockets on the river banks. Since the *Luftwaffe* would not be able to lend its full support to the battle on the Meuse until the following day, its bombers being needed elsewhere, it was vital that the Germans got as much armour as possible over to the left bank to meet an anticipated French counter-attack. When this developed, the French ran headlong into the tanks of the 1st *Panzer* Division, blasting its way into France, and in the brief, one-sided battle that followed the French lost eleven out of fifteen Hotchkiss light tanks.

The lightning speed and the relentless push of the German attack threw the French into total confusion. Frantic troops streamed back from the front with wild reports of masses of German armour converging on the French posts from all sides. Panic swept through the whole of the 55th and 71st Divisions, and the trickle of men abandoning their positions quickly became a flood. In fact, the rout began even before the first German tanks crossed the Meuse.

The total breakdown of morale spread through all sectors like an inferno and could not be stopped. Corps and Divisional headquarters, their lines of communication with the front shattered by the German bombing, were incapable of exercising the slightest control over the surging hysteria. On the morning of 14 May, the roads leading back from the Meuse were crammed with struggling columns of French troops, officers and men alike. In their haste to get away, they abandoned well-prepared defences, artillery batteries, rifles, webbing, sometimes even boots.

"*Sauve qui peut!*" the cry hung like a cloud over the retreating columns. French colonial African troops took it up and mimicked it, their accents turning the French words into "Shof ki po!"

Sauve qui peut; shof ki po. That was the motto of the French Army of the Meuse on this thirteenth day of May, 1940. Every man for himself.

Chapter Four

On the day after the German attack on Martigny the remainder of the Curtiss Hawk group moved to the airfield from its more usual location at Saint Dizier to be ready for large-scale escort missions over the Meuse. With it came the group commander, Colonel Villeneuve, a man bearing a celebrated name in the annals of French history. Lean and pipe-smoking, with a weatherbeaten face and thoughtful grey eyes that seemed to focus on something a long way off, Villeneuve had no hesitation in authorising Armstrong to fly with the group until such time as he could be returned to the RAF.

"We are short of pilots," he said, "and you seem to have acquired an aircraft for yourself. Perhaps we might discuss tactics to our mutual advantage?"

Armstrong hesitated to explain that he had been flying an unarmed photo-reconnaissance Spitfire for the past nine months, and that the fighter tactics he had learned on a frontline fighter squadron might now be out of date. From what he had seen so far, there didn't seem to be much difference between the combat formations used by the French and the British; both were much too tight to provide adequate room for manoeuvre, forcing the pilots to concentrate more on keeping station with one another than on keeping a good lookout. Like the RAF, the French used a 'weaver', a solitary aircraft bringing up the rear of the formation, weaving back and forth to keep an eye on the sky above and behind. Armstrong thought that there was little benefit in the method; all the weaver did was use up fuel faster than the other aircraft in the formation, and run the risk of being shot down first in the event of a 'bounce'. It would make far more sense to adopt a fluid fighter formation such as the Germans used, based on a pair of aircraft, with the number two watching out for the leader all the time. Two pairs of aircraft, flying in a formation that resembled the outspread fingertips of one's hand, could cover one another constantly, their pilots having a good view of all quarters of the sky.

Armstrong flew three sorties with the French during the next couple of days, and saw nothing. The action, it seemed, was further north; the RAF's Air Component, supporting the British Expeditionary Force, must be having a busy time. Then, early on the morning of 14 May, a grim-faced Villeneuve called all the pilots together for an open-air briefing. A map had been pinned to an easel and he referred to it now, pointing to the relevant places as he spoke.

"The enemy has broken through in strength here, at Sedan," he told the men. "The British are already attacking the pontoon bridges that have been erected across the Meuse, and have suffered many losses." He glanced briefly at Armstrong, who wondered how bad the losses really were.

"Now it is the turn of the French," Villeneuve continued. "The bridges and the troop concentrations in their vicinity will be attacked later this morning by eighteen Amiot 143 bombers from la Ferte-Gaucher and Nangis."

The pilots exchanged glances, and Armstrong knew why. The twin-engined Amiot 143, an angular, slab-sided aircraft that carried a crew of five, had already been out of date when it made its first flight in 1935. With a top speed that barely touched 150 miles per hour, it was completely unsuited to daylight operations against heavily-defended targets. If ever there was a suicide mission, this was it.

Villeneuve noticed their expressions. "I understand that all the bomber crews will be volunteers," he told them quietly. "Close fighter escort will be provided by twelve

Moranes, twelve Bloch 152s and nine Dewoitine 520s. We shall provide distant cover, and our task will be to keep the Messerschmitts at arm's length. Our orders are to patrol the Luxembourg border and intercept any enemy fighters heading for Sedan from the south-east; the RAF will be patrolling to the north. I need not tell you that we shall be close to the limit of our combat radius and that consequently it will be very important to conserve fuel. Take-off will be at 0800."

But the take-off was delayed, and delayed again, and it was well after eleven o'clock before the Hawks were ordered into the air. They formed up into four 'vics' of three, with Armstrong – very much the new boy as far as the French were concerned, despite his success over the airfield a couple of days earlier – flying on the right-hand side of the last formation. As they would not be flying fixed straight-line patrols in the combat area, Villeneuve had decided to dispense with the 'weaver'.

A hundred and fifty miles away, the lumbering Amiots had left their bases a while earlier and were cruising towards the target area. Over La Fère airfield they picked up their close escort of twelve Moranes; the other fighters were sweeping the sky a few minutes ahead, at high altitude.

Far to the south, Colonel Villeneuve took the Hawk formation up to 15,000 feet and crossed the Meuse, the fortress town of Verdun over on their left. Villeneuve brought the Hawks round in a gentle turn towards it, then flew north towards Luxembourg, twelve pairs of eyes anxiously scanning the sky. They saw nothing; but they could tell by the shouts and screams over their radios, tuned to the same frequency as those of the bombers and their escorts, that a murderous battle was developing in the sky over Sedan.

Just how murderous, they would not discover until later.

At 1215 the bombers and their escorts passed to the south of Mezières. A few minutes later they reached the

Meuse, and a turn to starboard brought them in towards Sedan from the north. So far, it was like a peacetime training flight; the sky was absolutely empty.

Suddenly, the air was filled with flak bursts and glowing trails of 20 mm shells. An Amiot was hit and began to drag a long ribbon of flame. It was an aircraft of Bomber Group II/34, and it carried the unit's commander, *Commandant* de Laubier. At the last moment, as the machine had been taxying out for take-off, de Laubier, defying orders to stay behind, had jumped aboard and taken the place of one of the gunners. Now, thirty minutes later, the other crews watched in horror as the Amiot plunged earthwards like a torch. Three of the crew bailed out and were taken prisoner; de Laubier was not among them.

At that moment the six aircraft of the second group, GB II/38, broke formation and turned in the direction of the Meuse bridges. The manoeuvre presented the fighter escort, which now had two separate formations to cover, with a problem. The Moranes split into two flights of six, one of which chased after II/38. The other six Amiots continued their run-in and unloaded their bombs on the congested roads north of Sedan, lurching as the flak hit them again and again. One machine turned away, trailing smoke, and began a descending turn towards friendly territory. Despite being attacked by an enemy fighter the pilot, Lieutenant Foucher, managed to regain his base after flying the whole way at treetop height.

As the bombers roared out of the flak zone, throttles wide open, the Messerschmitts pounced. A pair of Me 110s fastened themselves on to the tails of the surviving Amiots of II/34, one of which was quickly shot down in flames. The five-man crew bailed out. Another aircraft received three 20-mm shells in its port engine, which began to stream dense white smoke; a fourth shell shattered the port undercarriage, a fifth ripped the pilot's parachute pack to shreds and a sixth tore away the co-pilot's control column. The pilot, *Adjutant* Milan, made his escape into a bank of cloud and crash-landed in a field a few minutes later. The crew all got out safely, but the aircraft was a complete wreck.

By some miracle, all the other Amiots in the Sedan operation returned to base, although all of them were shot to ribbons and not one was in a battleworthy condition. Six Amiots, having failed to rendezvous with the fighter escort, had never reached the target area, but had turned back on the orders of their leader.

To the south, Colonel Villeneuve, incensed by the noise of battle over the radio and casting aside his earlier caution to save fuel, ordered his twelve fighters to head for Sedan at full throttle. Bringing up the rear, Armstrong felt a strong sense of unease; the turn towards Sedan had put them with their backs towards Germany, and he almost broke his neck as he swivelled his head from side to side, checking the dangerous sky astern.

When the action came, it came suddenly. There was a warning shout over the radio, and an instant later half a dozen Me 110s appeared dead ahead, diving steeply towards the haze that hung over the valleys far below. A gabble of excited French voices sounded over the air until Villeneuve's deep accent cut through them, telling them to shut up.

"Maintain formation," he ordered. "Do not attack. I repeat, do not attack."

His precise, matter-of-fact tone restrained the French pilots, who were clearly itching to dive after the 110s. It was just as well. A moment later, fifteen more 110s came diving out of the east, and were on top of the Hawks almost before the latter had time to react. Armstrong caught the flash of sunlight on their wings and identified them at once as they closed with the French fighters at terrific speed. Without waiting for orders he turned hard towards the threat, the force of gravity compressing him into his seat. His section leader, a young *sergent-chef* – the equivalent of an RAF flight sergeant – had the same idea and almost collided with Armstrong as he stood his aircraft on its wingtip.

A Messerschmitt slid into Armstrong's field of vision, closing rapidly from the starboard quarter. The German was firing in short bursts, the battery of cannon and machine-guns in its nose twinkling. Armstrong kept on turning towards it; it was the only thing to do. Suddenly, a cloud of smoke enveloped the enemy fighter's port engine and the 110 half-rolled and dropped away beneath. Armstrong never even saw the aircraft that had fired at it.

Another 110 appeared in front of Armstrong, weaving uncertainly from side to side, its crew clearly visible under their long transparent cockpit canopy. Armstrong kicked the rudder bar, his fingers pressing the twin triggers, and raked the Messerschmitt from wingtip to wingtip as it skidded through his sight. Its twin-finned tail broke away and whirled past him; the remainder dropped like a stone. He caught a glimpse of the German gunner trying to struggle clear before the 110 vanished.

He got in another burst at a 110 that fleeted across his nose, and then his guns jammed. With a pair of Messerschmitts turning hard to cut him off and no sign of any friendly fighters, he decided that it was time to make himself scarce. He pushed the Hawk's nose down, opened the throttle wide and dived hard towards the western side of the Meuse. The Hawk's acceleration in the dive was phenomenal and he easily outdistanced his pursuers, who followed him for some distance, firing a couple of ineffectual bursts, and then turned away.

Armstrong cleared the battle area and then, throttling back to husband his remaining fuel, found his way back to Martigny at low level, keeping a watchful eye on the sky to the rear all the way. He landed without incident and taxied in, switching off the engine and climbing stiffly from the cockpit. His ground crew looked at him expectantly, then broke into broad grins and clustered around him as he smiled and raised an index finger to indicate that he had destroyed an enemy aircraft.

"Only two more, *mon capitaine*, and you will be an ace," one of them said. Armstrong looked at him questioningly, and the man explained that under the French system of scoring victories, a pilot who destroyed five enemy aircraft was classed as an 'ace'; it was something that had come into being in the previous war. Armstrong shrugged; the RAF didn't bother with such a system, and never had done so. But then, you practically had to rip half a dozen enemy aircraft to shreds with your teeth before the RAF grudgingly gave you any recognition, let alone a medal. Perhaps it was better that way.

Armstrong told his ground crew about the problem with the guns, then went off to have a word with the intelligence officer, from whom he borrowed a cigarette – he normally smoked a pipe, but had no English tobacco with him and couldn't stand the aromatic French blends – and sat on the grass beside the dispersal hut to watch the others coming in. Villeneuve was among the first back. Presently, after a lengthy conversation with the intelligence officer, he strolled over to where Armstrong was sitting, fishing his pipe out of a pocket as he did so. The English pilot stood up as he approached. Villeneuve looked tired, and there was a deep frown on his forehead.

"So, my English friend, eight of us have returned. Two have landed elsewhere and two are missing. You destroyed a German, I understand. Well done. That makes three." He sighed and glanced up at the sky, over which some fleecy clouds were creeping.

"It is not enough. Not enough, by any means. We have to shoot down more of them. Our tactics are wrong. We need more fluidity, more freedom of action. The problem is, you see, that unlike your Royal Air Force, we are tied to the requirements of the army. We have no independence. We, the group and *escadrille* commanders, make representation to higher authority on how we might change things. We have done it many times since the start of the war, and we have been ignored just as often. If the Germans defeat us, God forbid, it will not be the fault of the pilots at the front."

Still frowning, he tamped tobacco into the bowl of his pipe and lit it before speaking again.

"The news is bad," he said. "I have just been informed that our French day bomber force is no longer capable of mounting attacks on the Meuse bridges. The losses have been too high. Which means, *mon ami*, that everything now depends on the RAF . . ."

Had Villeneuve and Armstrong but known it, the machinery that was to result in the martyrdom of the RAF's Advanced Air Striking Force had already been set in motion. In the early hours of that morning, General Billotte, commanding the French First Army Group, had telephoned Air Marshal Barratt and begged him to send the AASF into action in the Sedan area. "Victory or defeat hinges on the destruction of those bridges," the French general had emphasised. Barratt had accordingly authorised the AASF to attack the pontoons which the Germans had thrown across the Meuse, and the first two missions of this kind – carried out between 0430 and 0630 by ten Fairey Battles – had been encouraging, all the aircraft returning safely to base.

A few of the pontoons appeared to have been damaged, but Guderian's *panzers* continued to rumble across into the bridgehead established on the west bank the previous evening. Further north, the 6th *Panzer* Division pushed through a second breach in the Montherme area, while in the Dinant sector Erwin Rommel's 7th *Panzers* poured into a third bridgehead. Up to this point Air Vice-Marshal Playfair, the AASF's commander, had been holding the AASF in reserve to give his squadrons a few more hours in which to scrape together their available resources; these amounted to only sixty-two Battles and eight Blenheims, but with the French bomber force shot out of the sky by mid-morning Barratt and

Playfair had no alternative but to commit these battered remnants.

Between 1500 and 1600 that afternoon, the AASF threw every aircraft that could still fly into the cauldron. It was a massacre. No. 12 Squadron, which had already suffered heavily at Maastricht two days earlier, lost four aircraft out of five; No. 142 four out of eight; No. 226 three out of six; No. 105 six out of eleven; No. 150 lost all four; No. 88 one out of ten; No. 103 three out of eight and No. 218 ten out of eleven. Of the eight Blenheims sent out by 114 and 139 Squadrons, only three returned to base. It was the highest loss in an operation of similar size ever experienced by the RAF, and all that was achieved was the destruction of two pontoon bridges and the damaging of two more.

During the days that followed, six Battle crews, all shot down behind the enemy lines, managed to struggle back to their bases. They included a pilot who, although wounded in two places, somehow managed to swim the Meuse; and an observer and gunner who had stayed with their badly injured pilot in enemy territory for more than twenty-four hours, leaving him only when he died.

All the other crews – more than 100 young men – were either dead or prisoners.

At dusk, the pontoons were again attacked by twenty-eight Blenheims of No. 2 Group, from bases in England. Seven aircraft failed to return, including two which crashed in French territory.

The news of the disasters of 14 May, both in the air and on the ground, had a profound effect on the British War Cabinet's plans to send more aircraft, principally Hurricanes, to France . . .

HQ RAF FIGHTER COMMAND, BENTLEY PRIORY, 15 MAY 1940: 0900 HOURS

The tall, stern-faced man sat at his desk, frowning through half-moon spectacles at the memorandum he had recently drafted. He had just been ordered to dispatch a further 32 Hurricanes to the continent, and the French were pressing for an additional 120 machines. The memorandum, he knew, had to be correct in every word, for soon it would lie on the desk of the Prime Minister. He read it through again. He was a staid man, eccentric and alone. Would his words, he asked himself, have the necessary impact?

Sir,

I have the honour to refer to the very serious calls which have recently been made upon the Home Defence Fighter Units in an attempt to stem the German invasion of the Continent.

I hope and believe that our armies may yet be victorious in France and Belgium, but we have to face the possibility that they may be defeated.

In this case I presume that there is no one who will deny that England should fight on, even though the remainder of the Continent of Europe is dominated by the Germans.

For this purpose it is necessary to retain some minimum fighter strength in this country and I must request that the Air Council will inform me what they consider this minimum strength to be, in order that I may make my dispositions accordingly.

I would remind the Air Council that the last estimate which they made as to the force necessary to defend this country was fifty-two squadrons, and my strength has now been reduced to the equivalent of thirty-six squadrons.

Once a decision has been reached as to the limit on which the Air Council and the Cabinet are prepared to stake the existence of the country, it should be made clear to the Allied Commanders on the Continent that not a single aeroplane from Fighter Command beyond the limit will be sent across the Channel, no matter how desperate the situation may become.

It will, of course, be remembered that the estimate of fifty-two squadrons was based on the assumption that the attack would come from the eastwards except in so far as the defences might be outflanked in flight. We now have to face the possibility that attacks may come from Spain or even from the north coast of France. The result is that our line is very much extended at the same time as our resources are reduced.

I must point out that within the last few days the equivalent of ten squadrons have been sent to France, that Hurricane squadrons remaining in this country are seriously depleted, and that the more squadrons which are sent to France the higher will be the wastage and the more insistent the demand for reinforcements.

I must therefore request that as a matter of paramount urgency, the Air Ministry will consider and decide what level of strength is to be left to Fighter Command for the defence of this country, and will assure me that when this level has been reached, not one fighter will be sent across the Channel however urgent and insistent the appeals for help may be.

I believe that, if an adequate fighter force is kept in the country, if the fleet remains in being, and if Home Forces are suitably organized to resist invasion, we should be able to carry on the war single-handed for some time, if not indefinitely. But, if the Home Defence Force is drained away in desperate attempts to remedy the situation in France, defeat in France will involve the final, complete and irremediable defeat of this country.

H.C.T. Dowding,
Air Chief Marshal,
Air Officer Commanding-in-Chief
Fighter Command, Royal Air Force.

Dowding laid his glasses aside and rose from the desk, striding over to the window. His office faced south; he had chosen it especially for that reason, so that it would receive the sun for most of the day.

Bentley Priory stood on a ridge, four-square to the compass points. The Gothic building dated from the 1770s; it had successively been a stately home, an hotel and a girls' school before the Air Ministry bought it in 1926. It was a solid building, as solid as the English earth on which it stood. Soon, the destiny of Britain might be ordained within the walls of the Operations Room in the depths of the building, and by the courage of the Spitfire and Hurricane pilots of the thirty-six squadrons whose integrity Dowding was striving so desperately to preserve.

Too few, he thought. Too few. There will be great sacrifices. And as he gazed out on the trees in the park, without really seeing them, sadness mingled with the determination on his face.

BATTLE SITUATION:
ROTTERDAM, 14 MAY 1940

On the morning of 13 May, Major General Hubicki's 9th *Panzer* Division at last rolled over the Moerdijk bridge, cheered by its haggard defenders. The *Panzers* raced on through Dordrecht, and that evening they clattered into the outskirts of Rotterdam south of the Maas. Among the shattered houses near the southern end of the Willems bridge they ground to a halt, pinned down by heavy artillery fire. The paratroops were still clinging doggedly to their tenuous foothold on the northern end of the bridge. Their losses had been heavy, and the survivors were exhausted. They had been in action continuously for nearly four days. But there could be no question of withdrawing across the bullet-swept bridge to where the *Panzers* were waiting.

Command of the German forces in Rotterdam now rested on the shoulders of Rudolf Schmidt, General of the 39th Army Corps. His orders were to avoid unnecessary casualties among the Dutch civilians at all costs. On the evening of 13 May he therefore called on the Dutch commander, Colonel Scharroo, to surrender, pointing out that any further resistance would lead to widespread damage in the city and would only delay the inevitable capitulation by a few more hours.

But every one of those hours would mean a serious loss of time for the Germans. General von Kuchler, C-in-C of the 18th Army, feared that the British were on the point of landing an expeditionary force in Holland. The Dutch had to be broken quickly, for the German forces already committed against them were desperately needed for the push through Belgium into northern France. At 1900 on 13 May, von Kuchler therefore ordered that the Dutch resistance in Rotterdam was to be smashed by every available means. The battle plan envisaged a tank attack across the Willems bridge at 1530 the following afternoon, preceded by a large-scale air raid on the surrounding area to soften up the defenders.

By the morning of the 14th the Dutch commander still had not replied to General Schmidt's call for surrender. Two German envoys had been flown into the city to discuss capitulation terms. Eventually, at noon, they managed to make contact with Colonel Scharroo and deliver their ultimatum: surrender, or suffer the destruction of the city centre by the *Luftwaffe*. Scharroo found himself unable to make the decision alone; he told the envoys that he would have to get in touch with the Hague, the Dutch seat of government, for further instructions. Half an hour later, the Dutch Government replied that it was sending a delegation to Rotterdam to talk terms with the Germans. The deputation was due to arrive at 1400.

At 1330, General Schmidt sent a signal to *Luftflotte* 2 calling off the impending air attack, which was scheduled to begin at 1500. He was too late. At 1325, 100 Heinkels of KG 54 had taken off from their airfields near Bremen; by the time Schmidt's signal reached *Luftflotte* 2 the bombers were already approaching the Dutch border, and by the time the order to abort the raid filtered through to KG 54's HQ the Heinkels were over Holland. This meant that the radio operator in each aircraft had now closed down his position in order to take up his combat station behind the machine-gun in the blister beneath the fuselage.

The He 111s thundered towards Rotterdam in two waves. One, led by *Oberst* Lackner, KG 54's commanding officer, approached from the east; the other, headed by *Oberstleutnant* Hohne – commander of I/KG 54 – made a wide detour to attack from the south-west. Strapped to his knee each bomber pilot had a map of the city, with the Dutch-held zones at either end of the bridges outlined in red. It was precisely within these sectors that the crews had to place their bombs.

At 1505 Lackner's formation roared in over the outskirts of the city from the south, sailing through clusters of flak bursts. Lackner screwed up his eyes and searched for the target along the line of the river, which curved through Rotterdam in a sharp loop. It was hard to see anything at all; the city was shrouded in a veil of dusty haze and smoke through which the sun smouldered with a diffuse light. It was hardly surprising that the pilots never saw the red flares – the abort signal – which the German ground forces were sending up.

The Heinkels flew over the island in the middle of the Maas and unloaded their bombs in the centre of the Aldstadt, where the Dutch artillery was in position, then wheeled to starboard and vanished in the haze. A few seconds later, Hohne's formation came in from the south-west. In the cockpit of his Heinkel, Hohne concentrated on following the instructions of his bombardier as the latter guided him on to the target, where fires could be seen blazing fiercely amid piles of rubble.

Just as the bombardier pressed the release, Hohne caught an elusive glimpse of light above the Maas island. Straining his eyes, he saw it again: a red flare. He immediately pulled the Heinkel round in a 180-degree turn and the other pilots followed him, their bombs still on board.

Fifty-seven out of the hundred Heinkels of KG 54 – those of the first wave and Hohne's aircraft – had dropped a total of 100 bombs on Rotterdam, pulverising the city centre. Fire swept through the shattered streets, consuming everything in its path. A great pillar of smoke rose into the afternoon sky, darkening the sun. Beneath it lay the bodies of 814 Dutch civilians.

At 1700, just two hours after the attack, the Dutch garrison surrendered. At 1900, the *Panzers* rolled across the Maas bridges watched by the airborne troops, who were too exhausted to raise a cheer.

This was Western Europe in May 1940. This was total war.

Chapter Five

Colonel Villeneuve was writing his daily report. He was desperately weary, and his hand trembled a little as he penned the words. The Hawks had been in almost continuous action for the past forty-eight hours, and all the pilots were feeling the strain.

Thursday, 16 May 1940. Early this morning the *Groupe* moved to a new airfield at Orconte, near Saint-Dizier, with seven serviceable Hawks – all we have left out of a complement of thirty-four. While we were establishing ourselves at our new location, we were briefed to fly an air cover mission south-west of Charleroi. Take-off was fixed for 1100. All seven available aircraft were to take part. The pilots were selected from the 3rd and 4th *Escadrilles*: *Lieutenant* Vincotte, *Sous-Lieutenant* Baptizet, *Sous-Lieutenant* Plubeau and *Adjutant* Tesseraud from the 4th, *Capitaine* Guieu, *Capitaine* Armstrong (RAF) and *Sergent-Chef* Casenobe from the 3rd.

We climbed without incident until we were over Reims, when we saw a superb V of nine twin-engined bombers heading south-west at 4,000 metres. We decided to attack. They were escorted by half a dozen Me 109s, 1,000 metres higher up and a little behind. *Lieutenant* Vincotte attacked, perhaps a little too soon. The Messerschmitts came down on our aircraft and the pilots were forced to break away and dive for safety. Only *Lieutenant* Vincotte stuck to the bombers and made several passes at the left-hand one (a Junkers 88). Meanwhile, Plubeau,

Tesseraud and Baptizet were involved in a fierce dogfight with the 109s; each shot down an enemy fighter and then climbed rapidly to the aid of Vincotte. Together, they shot down one bomber; the remainder dropped their bombs haphazardly near Warmeriville and we went after them.

Plubeau's cockpit was shattered by an explosive shell and he was forced to bail out. Vincotte damaged a second Junkers, then he too was hit in the fuel tanks and also had to bail out as his cockpit was filling with fumes and his oxygen equipment was out of action.

Meanwhile, Guieu, Armstrong and Casenobe had spotted a Henschel 126 at low altitude, which they attacked and shot down in the forest of Silly-l'Abbaye. In the process Armstrong flew through a treetop at full throttle; by some miracle he managed to reach base and land safely with great gashes torn in his wings. Our Englishman, it seems, bears a charmed life.

Villeneuve laid aside his pen for a moment and rubbed his eyes, resting his elbows on the trestle table that served as a desk. At that moment, the Englishman in question came into the tent that Villeneuve was using as his office, failing better accommodation. Armstrong saluted; the French officer waved a hand in reply and pointed to a chair. He reached for a half-empty bottle of wine, inspected it by holding it up so that the light of the solitary oil lamp shone through it, and filled two glasses, one of which he handed to Armstrong. Villeneuve raised his glass and gave a lop-sided smile.

"Well then, let's drink to treetops," he said. "I trust you have recovered from your experience?"

"It isn't one I wish to repeat in a hurry," Armstrong admitted. "I still don't know how I got away with it."

The Henschel, a high-wing army co-operation machine similar to the RAF's Westland Lysander, had been chugging along sedately at 500 feet, doubtless spying out the land for the approaching *Panzers*, when Armstrong and the others had pounced on it. Armstrong, intent on delivering a killing burst of fire, had misjudged his speed badly and had almost collided with the enemy aircraft, which by then had decended almost to ground level. Forced to break away sharply, he had not even seen the tree that did all the damage until it was too late.

"The aircraft is just about fit to fly again," he added. "The boys have been working on it all day."

"Then that gives us five serviceable aircraft for the morning," Villeneuve commented. "Five! And there are rows of brand-new fighters, Dewoitines, sitting outside the factory at Toulouse because no one will take it upon himself to sign the necessary paperwork so that they can be released to the frontline squadrons. It is criminal, Armstrong. Criminal!" The Frenchman sighed in resignation and reached for his pipe.

While Villeneuve lit up, Armstrong reflected on the day's other events, or at least those he knew about. If Villeneuve's *Groupe* had taken a beating, the *Escadrille* that shared the airfield with it, a Morane 406 squadron, had fared even more badly. Nine of them had taken off that afternoon and had been attacked by twelve Me 109s over Charleroi; using their comfortable margin of speed to good advantage – they were about 60 miles per hour faster than the French fighters – the 109s had flown round the Moranes in a circle some 5,000 feet higher up and attacked in pairs, afterwards zooming up to altitude once more. With the 109s' first passes two Moranes went down in flames; neither pilot bailed out.

More 109s arrived on the scene and the remaining Moranes soon found themselves attacked by three or four adversaries each. A third French fighter went down in flames and this time the pilot managed to bail out, although he was seriously wounded. A fourth pilot, his Morane riddled with shells, crash-landed on the airfield at Soissons, his aircraft a total wreck. A fifth pilot was hit in the head by shell splinters while racing for safety at treetop height and lost consciousness; when he came to he found that his aircraft had made a perfect wheels-up landing in a field. Only four Moranes had returned from the sortie.

Everywhere, Armstrong reasoned, it must be the same story. The *Luftwaffe* ruled the sky over the battle front. He wondered what the true situation was, and how quickly the collapse was taking place.

Armstrong had no way of knowing it, but the situation in eastern France had only just been made brutally clear to a very important person who had arrived in Paris at four o'clock that afternoon aboard a de Havilland Flamingo airliner, having taken off from London an hour earlier. After a preliminary briefing at the British Embassy, Winston Churchill, Prime Minister for only five days, had gone on to the Quai d'Orsay for a meeting with the French Premier, Paul Reynaud. The previous day, Reynaud had telephoned Churchill with a grim message. "We have been defeated. We are beaten; we have lost the battle. The front is broken near Sedan . . ."

We are beaten. Every man for himself. *Sauve qui peut*. The mentality of defeat had penetrated the inner circle of the French Government . . .

When Churchill arrived at the Quai d'Orsay, accompanied by General Lord Ismay, head of the Military Wing of the War Cabinet Secretariat, and General Dill, Vice-Chief of the Imperial General Staff, he was confronted by the sight of French civil servants making bonfires of government archives in the grounds. Already, they were preparing to evacuate the capital.

Churchill and his companions were conducted to a magnificent conference room where Reynaud was waiting to receive him. Edouard Daladier, the Minister of National Defence and War, and General Gamelin were also present. Churchill noted utter dejection written on all their faces.

With the aid of a map mounted on an easel, Gamelin explained the battle situation. The Germans had broken through to the north and south of Sedan, and the French Army in that sector was destroyed or scattered. Enemy armoured columns were pushing on with great speed towards Amiens and Arras, apparently with the intention of reaching the Channel coast in the region of Abbeville and driving a wedge between the Allied armies. Alternatively, Gamelin thought, they might make for Paris. Behind the armour came eight or ten German motorised infantry divisions, steadily widening the gap as they pushed through the two dislocated French armies on either side.

When Gamelin stopped talking, there was a long silence. Then Churchill, in his barely understandable French, asked: *"Ou est la masse de manoeuvre* – where is the strategic reserve?"

Gamelin's reply was a shake of the head, a shrug, and a single word. *"Aucune."* None. There was no reserve.

Churchill was visibly shocked. Suddenly, he had come face to face with the appalling shortcomings of the French High Command. With 500 miles of front to defend, they had left themselves with no insurance against an enemy breakthrough – no divisions with which to launch a strong counter-offensive once the first fury of the enemy attack had spent itself.

To make matters worse, the British had never been informed of this deficiency, even though the British Expeditionary Force was serving under French command. But Gamelin, despite his evident despair, was not yet finished. He began to speak of the possibility of striking at the flanks of the German advance, using divisions withdrawn from the Maginot Line to the south. There were two or three armoured divisions which had not yet been engaged. Eight or nine more divisions were being brought from North Africa, and would arrive in the battle zone within two or three weeks ... suddenly, both the general and his argument collapsed. With another shrug of the shoulders, he complained about inferiority of numbers, inferiority of equipment, inferiority of tactics. And where were the British, with only ten divisions in Europe after eight months of war? Where were the additional promised squadrons of the Royal Air Force?

Fighters were needed not only to give cover to the French Army, but also to stop the German tanks.

Churchill was vehemently opposed to this idea. "No!" he objected. "It is the business of the artillery to stop the tanks. The business of the fighters is to *nettoyer le ciel*, to cleanse the skies over the battle."

That morning, Churchill's Cabinet had given him authority to move four more squadrons of Hurricanes to France. Now, at the close of the meeting with Gamelin, he sent a telegram to the Cabinet to ask for the despatch of six more. The reply came shortly before midnight, when Churchill was being entertained at Reynaud's apartment. Approval was given for the despatch of ten fighter squadrons in total.

Six squadrons were assembled on airfields in Kent, within easy reach of the Continent. It was arranged that every morning, three squadrons would cross over to France, operate from French bases until midday, and return to England after being replaced by three more. But, much to Air Chief Marshal Dowding's relief, the squadrons were never based permanently on French soil.

Events were happening much too swiftly for that.

Chapter Six

The weariness clutched at every fibre of Armstrong's body. He had flown five sorties since dawn; now, at six o'clock in the evening, grimy and unshaven, his body clammy with the sweat that had poured from him as he sweltered under the hot May sun in his fighter's cockpit, he wanted nothing more than to bathe some of the tension away, snatch something to eat and fall into a coma.

He had lost count of the days. Today was 20 May, he thought, but without looking it up on the calendar he couldn't be sure. The day before, the *Groupe* – its complement increased to eight aircraft with the arrival of some replacements, the survivors of another unit that had been decimated in the fighting – had moved again, this time to Anglure, north of the Seine, from where it had operated almost continuously in support of a doomed French counter-offensive aimed at preventing the Germans breaking through the Oise valley.

Armstrong had seen the failure of the counter-offensive for himself, etched in the smoke of burning French tanks as, high above, the French fighter squadrons had striven desperately to keep the *Luftwaffe* at bay.

On 17 May the Germans had crossed the River Sambre and by nightfall had penetrated the Forest of Mormal. The French counter-attack had not started until the evening of the 19th, having been delayed because of the difficulty in moving troops and equipment up to the jump-off point under constant air attack. In the small hours the attacking force reached its first objective, the railway line running between Berlaimont and Le Quesnoy, but the Germans rapidly reinforced their troops and succeeded in surrounding the French right flank near Englefontaine. By this time the French armoured support had collapsed through lack of fuel, and it was only with the greatest difficulty that General Mesny, the French commander, managed to extricate most of his forces from the rapidly closing trap.

That morning, Armstrong and his fellow pilots had flown two sorties in response to a desperate plea for help by the French 43rd Division, which had abandoned its positions and begun the march westwards. The move had been forestalled by a heavy German attack on the French fortified positions at Bavai, and the remaining seven battalions of the 43rd had found themselves involved in fierce fighting.

The fighter pilots had strafed the Germans until their ammunition had run out, but they had been unable to stave off the inevitable. One by one, the 43rd's battalions had been annihilated, except for a few men who managed to get away. The 10th *Chasseurs* battalion, forming the rearguard, was assailed by a whole German infantry regiment. The *Chasseurs* fought on until their ammunition was exhausted, then they burned their colours, fixed bayonets and charged the enemy. To a man, they were mown down by the German machine-guns.

On 17 May, with the aid of five divisions which had just reached the front, the French had attempted to form a new field army to block the Germans' advance along the Oise. Even at this stage, the French General Staff still believed that they had enough tanks left to launch a strong armoured counter-attack; in reality, the only armoured formation at their disposal was the embryo 4th Division, with two scratch battalions. This lay in the open country between the forward elements of General Guderian's 1st *Panzer* Division and the River Oise, and was commanded by a tall, dignified tank officer, a certain Colonel Charles de Gaulle.

The first objective of de Gaulle's two weakened and under-strength armoured brigades was the village of Montcornet, which had recently been captured by Guderian and commanded a strategic position astride the crossroads leading to Saint Quentin, Laon and Reims. The 6th Brigade approached the objective from Laon, following the left flank of the road, while on the right the 8th Brigade passed through Boncourt and Ville aux Bois, each column followed by a detachment of the 2nd Dismounted Dragoons and some groups of *Chasseurs*.

After a preliminary skirmish, the attack against Montcornet was launched in daylight and de Gaulle's tanks penetrated into the outskirts of the village. With only one battalion of *Chasseurs* to support them, however, they could not hold on and were compelled to withdraw after destroying a single German tank. De Gaulle's forces were pulled back, attacked by German aircraft all the way, and found shelter in the Forest of Samoussy between Sissonne and Bruyeres. The colonel summed up the situation to his staff officers in a single sentence.

"We are like lost children thirty kilometres in front of the Aisne," he told them.

The situation brightened a little on 18 May with the arrival of some reinforcements, including forty Somua tanks of the 3rd *Cuirassiers*. The new arrivals came just in time, for by the morning of the 18th the 4th Division had only sixty tanks left, twenty of which were heavy 33-ton 'B' types. On the 19th, with the aid of these reinforcements, de Gaulle was ordered to cross the River Serre and attack Guderian's lines of communication.

The attack was launched at 0700, the French tanks moving forward in three parallel columns, but by this time the Germans had had ample opportunity to mine the approaches to the Serre bridges and bring up their anti-tank batteries, and before the attack had been under way half an hour, the *Stukas* appeared in full strength. By 0900 de Gaulle's thrust had ground to a halt, while on its right flank the supporting infantry were attacked again and again by bombers and German tanks, followed by infantry assault groups.

Desperate to hold on for as long as possible, the 4th Armoured Division's infantry clung to their positions just short of Laon and suffered further attacks throughout the night, finally extricating themselves with great difficulty the next morning.

The gallant failure of de Gaulle's small counter-offensive marked the French Army's last chance to blunt the German advance with the use of armour. As Armstrong and the other pilots were climbing wearily from their aircraft at the end of the day's last sortie, what was left of the French 4th Division was pulling back across the Aisne.

The pilots sat on the grass or in deckchairs near the dispersal hut, despairing now of a proper evening meal. Everything was in chaos, and they had to be content with bread and cheese, washed down by black coffee dispensed by a couple of orderlies. They chewed on their food mechanically, speaking in monosyllables between mouthfuls. Having finished, some wandered off to their tents, dog-tired, while others stayed where they were to smoke a last cigarette before turning in. Nobody took much notice when a telephone bell shrilled inside the hut.

Armstrong rose stiffly to his feet and was about to wander off to bed when Villeneuve emerged from the hut, looking perplexed, and caught sight of him. The day before, he had made Armstrong a flight commander; the Englishman was now one of the *Groupe*'s senior surviving pilots and has passed the five-victory mark which made him, as the French called it, an 'ace'.

"There's something odd going on, Armstrong," Villeneuve said. "Here we are in the thick of things, and suddenly I've been ordered to take all available aircraft to Le Bourget – that's the civil airport at Paris, as you may know – first thing tomorrow morning. I'm supposed to report to a

Commandant Daurat. I knew someone of that name years ago. If it's the same fellow, he's a transport pilot. I wonder what it's all about?"

"Perhaps they're going to give us all some leave," grinned a nearby pilot, who had overheard. "Give us a chance to dip our wicks, one last time, before—" He made a cutting motion across his throat with the edge of his hand. Villeneuve ignored him, being preoccupied with the orders he had just received. At length, he said:

"We shall know soon enough. In the meantime, get some sleep. We shall all need to be up before dawn." He glanced towards the north-east, where the rumble of artillery fire could be heard. "Closer," he murmured to himself. "Always closer. God knows, sleep may be hard enough to come by."

Armstrong slept, undisturbed by the noise of the guns, but he awoke feeling far from refreshed. He knew that he must have been dreaming again, although he could not recall what the dream might have been. He had experienced a recurring dream during the past two or three nights, an odd dream in which he had been imprisoned in a small room, struggling to get to the chink of light that revealed some sort of entrance, but prevented from doing so by mounds of jigsaw puzzles, broken up into their component pieces and piled in his path like miniature mountains. Most tired pilots who had been in action, he knew, dreamed about combat, of being chased by dogged enemy fighters or of being trapped in burning aircraft. Not him; he dreamed about bloody jigsaw puzzles. Perhaps he was going round the bend.

Shaking his head, he crawled out of his one-man tent stark naked. Some of the Frenchmen, he knew, had taken to sleeping in their clothes in case they had to make a hurried departure, but Armstrong refused to follow their example. He felt scruffy enough as it was, with yesterday's sweat and grime dried upon his skin.

The morning air was cool, with just enough chill in it

to clutch at the back of his throat as he took his first deep breath. He blinked against the red, molten ball of the sun, its upper rim just beginning to poke over the horizon. There were tendrils of haze across it, but whether they were caused by drifting smoke or the natural mists of early morning he had no means of telling. He stood there for a few moments, inhaling to clear his head. He would have liked nothing more than to go for a short run – his morning habit for years now – but he knew that there would be no time. Instead, he dived briefly back into his tent and re-emerged clutching his razor – still the same one that had been given to him by Madame Bessodes an eternity ago – a grimy towel and a cake of soap.

There was a water-filled trough at some distance from his tent, and he was glad to see that he was the first there; no soapy scum was floating on the surface. Bending down, he splashed freezing water over his head, leaving his face wet, and rubbed the cake of soap around his jawline. Then he dipped his shaving brush into the water and set about trying to work up some sort of lather, a task accompanied by only partial success. This was one morning ritual that caused great amusement among his French colleagues, most of whom had not shaved for days. It didn't seem to have affected their performance in action. Armstrong shaved carefully, allowing an interval of a minute or two before putting the razor to his face. He had found by accident that if you left your face wet for a while, shaving with cold water presented no problems – why, he had no idea. But when he had finished his face was smooth and unnicked, and he felt a lot better as he dried himself down after washing all over.

Within minutes the other pilots were up and about, breakfasting on bread, sausage and steaming black coffee while the mechanics tested the engines of the Hawks. The valiant ground crews had worked all night to make the aircraft serviceable, repairing battle damage, and must have been fit to drop. Armstrong noticed that everyone

82

glanced surreptitiously at the eastern sky from time to time, as though expecting an enemy air attack to materialise at any moment. He reflected that they had been lucky so far. The luck could not possibly last.

The flight to Paris took only a few minutes, the eight Hawks landing on schedule at Le Bourget. Colonel Villeneuve discovered to his delight that he and *Commandant* Daurat were indeed old acquaintances, and that Daurat was commander of the French GHQ Transport Flight. Villeneuve asked him what the score was, and was amazed when the other spread his hands wide in perplexity.

"I have no idea, *mon Colonel*," he said apologetically. "I know only that I had a telephone call from a GHQ staff officer yesterday evening, who told me to prepare a fast bomber for a vital mission this morning and to provide a fighter escort. Yours was the *Groupe* best placed for that task. The problem, as I quickly discovered, was that no bomber was available. At length, in desperation, I telephoned a friend at the Air Force test centre at Saint-Inglevert and he asked the CO there if a machine could be spared. There was only one, an Amiot 354."

This, Villeneuve was aware, was France's finest and fastest bomber. It had not yet entered service and was still undergoing its trials. For the test centre to spare it, something really important must be in the wind.

At that moment, a messenger roared up on a motorcycle and addressed Daurat. A general had arrived on the airfield; he was waiting in Daurat's office and was not, it seemed, in a particularly pleasant mood. Daurat jumped on the pillion and sped away towards the operations room; Villeneuve and his pilots stayed where they were, wondering what was going to happen next.

While they waited, they watched with interest as a brand new Amiot 354 landed and taxied in. It parked close to the fighters, the polished metal of its wings and fuselage contrasting sharply with the drab camouflage of the other aircraft. Three crew members climbed from the Amiot, and the pilot came over to introduce himself to Villeneuve. His name was *Capitaine* Henri Lafitte, and he was a test pilot. Like Villeneuve, he was completely in the dark about the true nature of the mission.

"It must be something important, though," he said. "We've been armed, especially for the occasion."

Villeneuve glanced at the bomber, and saw twin machine-guns protruding from the rear turret. He also saw that Lafitte was grinning, and raised a questioning eyebrow.

"They're wooden dummies," Lafitte told him. "They look realistic enough, but I don't suppose for a moment that they would fool the *Boches*."

Their attention was diverted by the approach of a staff car. It halted a few yards away; Daurat got out and opened the rear door. Villeneuve brought his pilots quickly to attention as he spotted the gold braid of a general's *kepi*. A moment later he let out a gasp as he recognised the occupant. Armstrong glanced sideways at him. "It's Weygand," Villeneuve murmured. The name meant nothing to the Englishman; but it was a name that would become very familiar to the Allies in the days to come. General Maxime Weygand, Commander-in-Chief of all French forces on land, at sea and in the air.

Weygand. Despite his seventy-three years, he bore himself with pride and youthful vigour. His cheeks were hollow, but his eyes were bright and piercing, his mouth set in a firm line. He might have been one of Napoleon's generals, stepping from a page of history when all Europe lay at France's feet, instead of an old man summoned from across the sea in a desperate bid to rally the tottering French armies and exhort them to stand firm against the *Panzers* that were debouching across the plains of Flanders. This was the man who, nearly a quarter of a century earlier, had been the shadow of the great Marshal Foch; it was Weygand who had been at Foch's right hand on that fateful day in November 1918, when the Armistice terms had been presented to the defeated Germans in the Marshal's special train at Compiègne.

His critics – and there had been many – had often cast doubt on his powers of leadership, drawing strength from the fact that he had never commanded troops in battle. In 1920 he had been sent to Poland as France's representative on an Allied mission whose task had been to advise the Poles in their fight against the invading Russians, and there were those who claimed that he had been the mastermind behind the Polish success. Two years after his return to France he had been appointed high commissioner to Syria, and in 1931 he had been elevated to the post of Commander-in-Chief, French Army.

In 1939, after four years of retirement, he had been recalled to the colours and sent back to Syria as military commander. He was still there on 10 May 1940, when the Germans launched their offensive against France and the Low Countries. On the eighteenth he had been in Cairo, conferring with General Wavell, the British commander in Egypt, when an urgent signal arrived from French Premier Paul Reynaud summoning him to Paris.

He left immediately, hoping that the aircraft would reach Paris that same evening after refuelling at Tunis. The machine, however, encountered strong headwinds and the pilot was forced to turn back and refuel at Mersa Matruh in Egypt, losing three precious hours. His homecoming seemed to be dogged by misfortune; when the aircraft finally touched down in France on the morning of the nineteenth, at Etampes airfield, its undercarriage collapsed and Weygand had to scramble clear through a gun turret, shaken but otherwise unhurt.

He arrived at Vincennes, the French GHQ, at 1530 that same day, and had an interview with the Commander-in-Chief, General Maurice Gamelin – the unhappy man who was about to be made the scapegoat for the series of military disasters that had overwhelmed the French armies in the field during the past week. It was only then, in the course of Gamelin's briefing, that Weygand had begun to appreciate the full magnitude of these disasters and the dire peril that confronted his nation.

That evening, Weygand had a meeting with Paul Reynaud and Marshal Philippe Pétain, who at Reynaud's invitation had joined the government as deputy premier twenty-four hours earlier. After some preliminary discussion, Reynaud asked Weygand to take over the reins from Gamelin. After pondering for a while, the ageing general said:

"Very well. I accept the responsibility you are placing on me. You will not be surprised if I do not promise victory, or even give you hope of a victory." On this far from optimistic note, he retired for his first real sleep since leaving North Africa.

He was back in the C-in-C's office at Vincennes early the next morning, looking much refreshed. There was a brief, cool meeting with Gamelin, during which the latter formally handed over to his replacement. Afterwards Gamelin left Vincennes for ever, a solitary and pathetic figure, bidding goodbye to no one.

Weygand knew that his first task must be to confer with all the Allied commanders and work out a speedy and co-ordinated plan of action. He believed, rightly, that the Allied forces north of the corridor that was being driven towards the Channel coast by the *Panzers* were now in a critical position; it was becoming clear that the enemy planned first to eliminate these forces by crushing them between the hammer and anvil of their two Army Groups before swinging south into the heartland of France.

But Weygand did not really know what was happening to the Allied armies in the north, for all direct communications had been severed by the rapid advance of the enemy, and any news that trickled through to Vincennes came second-hand, via the link with London. Weygand therefore send urgent signals to King Leopold of the Belgians, to General Billotte, commanding the French First Army Group, and to General

Gort, commander of the BEF, requesting a meeting at Ypres on the afternoon of 21 May. His original plan had been to travel to Abbeville by train, and from there to Ypres; but Abbeville was already within sight of Guderian's armoured spearheads, so the only alternative was to fly to Ypres by means of the fastest available aircraft.

So Weygand snatched a few hours' sleep at Vincennes, having finalised the arrangements for the flight north the next morning – or so he thought. Arriving at Le Bourget, he made a brief inspection of the assembled pilots, expressing surprise at finding Armstrong among them and exchanging a few words with him after Villeneuve had explained the reason for the Englishman's presence. Running through Wegand's mind was the cornerstone of the plan he had been working on: an armoured attack by the British on the flanks of the German advance at Arras.

So much, he thought, depended on the British, who had been conducting a magnificent fighting withdrawal back from the river Dyle to set up a new line of defence on the Escaut. There was no rout there, no panic-stricken retreat; only good order and discipline. And yet Weygand knew that many of the British troops were not regular soldiers at all, but part-time territorials . . .

Weygand turned to Lafitte and asked him if all was ready for the forthcoming mission. The pilot of the Amiot bomber looked bewildered.

"*Mon general*", he confessed, "I have no idea what the mission is to be. I have received no orders, other than that I was to report here with all speed."

Sudden anger flashed across Weygand's face. Calming himself with some difficulty, for this state of affairs only served to confirm the confusion that prevailed everywhere, he asked for a map. Somebody produced one, and Weygand held an impromptu briefing, working out the details of the flight with Lafitte and Villeneuve.

First of all they would set course for Abbeville, following the valley of the Somme, then turn towards Cambrai or

Valenciennes. They would then make a reconnaissance of the Lens-Béthune area, landing at Norrent-Fontes airfield to refuel. GHQ had arranged for Weygand to be picked up there and taken by road to Ypres for his meeting with the Allied commanders. Altitude for the flight was to be 2,500 feet, out of range of enemy small-arms fire and below the effective level of most medium and heavy flak. Strict radio silence was to be maintained, unless of course the Amiot and its escorts were attacked.

Weygand's Amiot took off at exactly 0900, the eight fighters of the escort slipping protectively into place above it and on either side. The sky was cloudless, with near-perfect visibility.

Beauvais airfield slid by underneath their wings. Glancing down, Armstrong saw smoke drifting from it, indicating that it had been under recent attack. A couple of minutes later, he spotted three Dornier 17s, escorted by a dozen Me 110s, above and to the right, and turned the safety catch of his guns to 'fire' in anticipation of trouble; but the enemy formation maintained a steady course towards the south and was soon lost to sight.

The town of Poix slipped by on the starboard side, and now the pilots began to see signs of war. The autoroute leading south from the town was jammed solid with vehicles of every description, ranging from heavy lorries to horse-drawn carts; a terror-driven exodus was under way. The scene of confusion fell astern as the aircraft droned over the lush, dark green landscape of the Somme valley. Ahead of them a haze of smoke hung over the horizon; underneath it lay Abbeville, and heavy fighting seemed to be going on around the town. The sight came as an unpleasant shock to the pilots, who had not realised that the *Panzers* had advanced so far. The roads beneath were once again congested, this time with armour and military transport. The stark black crosses on the roofs and turrets of the vehicles left no doubt as to their identity.

The aircraft turned north-east towards Arras. Tracer

drifted up lazily from a concentration of enemy armour, and a moment later clusters of black puffs burst around the formation as 20-mm mobile flak batteries opened up. Splinters ripped through the Amiot, a few feet from where Weygand was sitting at the navigator's plotting table, intent on his maps. He did not trouble to raise his head. Lafitte opened the throttles and the bomber surged forward, leaving the danger behind.

The formation passed to the south of Arras, over more military convoys. Although fires were burning here and there, the town itself seemed quiet and there was no sign of fighting. Cambrai, a few miles further on, presented a different picture. The centre of the town was in flames and fighting appeared to be in progress in the surrounding countryside, although the drifting pall of smoke made it hard to see exactly what was happening. A lot of flak started to come up and the formation turned west, heading for Norrent-Fontes, near the Belgian border.

The Amiot touched down without incident on Norrent-Fontes airfield while the fighter escort circled watchfully overhead. Then the fighters came in; one's undercarriage refused to come down and the pilot made a belly landing, climbing unhurt from the cockpit. He would have to continue his journey in the bomber.

Villeneuve, worried now that his fighters were reduced to seven in number, went over to where Weygand and the bomber crew were standing beside their machine. The general was in a towering rage. GHQ had informed him that an air force group was still based here; it turned out that it had departed three days earlier. Norrent-Fontes' only inhabitant was a small and incredibly scruffy private, who now stood off to one side looking overawed by the close proximity of so much gold braid. When the group left, he had been told to stay behind and look after the airfield's fuel dump pending further orders. The orders had not arrived, but he had stolidly remained at his post, not knowing what else to do. Villeneuve accompanied him to the fuel dump; it contained 20,000 litres, stacked in 20-litre drums. The pilots descended on it and were soon hard at work refuelling their machines.

Meanwhile, Weygand and his aide had set off in search of a telephone, driven by the little soldier in a decrepit truck that was the airfield's sole remaining mode of transport. All the telephones on the aerodrome were out of action, but they found one in a post office in a nearby village, from where Weygand managed to contact First Army Group. Over a badly distorted line, he learned that General Billotte had sent out cars to search for him. The problem was that no one knew where he might be.

Back at Norrent-Fontes, the pilots were awaiting Weygand's return. Suddenly, a car drove up in a cloud of dust and screeched to a halt. A French army officer jumped out. The man seemed panic-stricken.

"What are you doing here?" he cried. "The *Boches* are only ten kilometres away, and they're advancing at sixty kilometres an hour. Get out, while you still can."

Villeneuve asked the man if he had seen anything of Weygand. The officer became even more agitated.

"How am I supposed to recognise anyone in this shambles? If he's gone towards Hazebrouck he's been taken prisoner, that's for sure. Go on, get out! You haven't much time."

The officer ran back to his car and drove off at high speed. The pilots looked at one another, torn by uncertainty. What if Weygand had been taken prisoner, and the Germans were as close as the staff officer had indicated? At any moment the *Stukas* might appear overhead and blast their aircraft into smoking wreckage.

They waited for twenty minutes, their nerves in knots. Villeneuve was about to give the order to take off when a vehicle came lurching past the hangars; it was the little soldier's truck. Weygand and his aide got out, the general white-faced and in obvious distress.

"Colonel," he said to Villeneuve, "the situation is lamentable. I had never dreamed that such chaos existed. The roads are so clogged that movement is almost impossible. We must keep cool, or we're finished."

He pondered for a few moments, poring over his map. Finally, he decided to take off for the airfield at Saint-Inglevert, near Calais. It was just possible that the transport sent out by Billotte might be waiting for him there.

The formation was airborne by noon. A few minutes later the pilots sighted the Channel, with Boulogne over on the left. Armstrong noticed a forest of barrage balloons over the port. With Calais dead ahead the formation let down slowly towards Saint-Inglevert, the Amiot landing first. It was only as he made his approach to land that Armstrong saw that the airfield was pitted with bomb craters. It was a miracle that Weygand's bomber, which needed a fairly long landing run, had managed to touch down without wrecking itself.

Weygand came over and shook each pilot by the hand. He instructed them to wait for him until 1900 hours; if he had not returned by that time they were to fly back to Le Bourget. Then the general set off into Calais in a car his aide had somehow managed to commandeer.

The pilots pushed their aircraft into the shelter of a bombed-out hangar and settled down to wait, smoking nervously. From time to time formations of German bombers cruised overhead, their passage followed by the drum-roll of explosions in Calais.

The appointed time came, and there was no sign of Weygand. The pilots waited for another hour, then took off and set course for Paris. Their mission was over; what had become of the general was no longer their concern. It was enough that they had got through the day unscathed, with the exception of the Curtiss on its belly at Norrent-Fontes.

Sitting on one of his fuel drums, the little soldier watched them go. He was still sitting there, under the stars, when German tanks rolled onto the airfield. German soldiers, poking fun at his scruffy appearance and undernourished physique, gave him some bread and soup and then marched him off into captivity. They couldn't understand why he was smiling beatifically, as though he had seen a vision.

The little soldier survived the war, and afterwards opened up a wine shop in Boulogne. A very old man now, he still likes to sit outside in the sun at his ease, for the business is run by his sons and their families.

For the price of a drink, although his sons disapprove, he will tell you how he was once kissed on the cheeks by no less a person than General Maxime Weygand and commended for his great gallantry under fire while acting as the general's driver. He was promised a medal. And he will tell you about the brave pilots, who flew away to certain death in the defence of France after he, and he alone, provided them with petrol for their aeroplanes.

Of course, the story has become a little embellished with the passage of years, and the old man regrets that he cannot show you the promised medal, which he never received.

C'est la guerre.

Chapter Seven

Armstrong was exceedingly drunk. They were all exceedingly drunk, oblivious to everything but the table at which they sat, its top covered with bottles of wine. The noise and the smoke of the bar cocooned them pleasantly, forming a strange silence of its own. Only they mattered, only they existed in their little universe. Outside was not there, and to hell with tomorrow.

Forty-eight glorious hours, that was what Villeneuve had won for them. Of what use, he had protested to Air HQ, was a squadron of pilots so tired that they were falling asleep in their cockpits? What sense did it make, to go on throwing themselves into combat day after day, without proper rest, while other squadrons in the south had barely seen action?

Only five of them were left now, apart from Villeneuve, who had gone off on some errand, leaving them to savour the delights of Paris. And savour them they had, from top to bottom, and the greatest delight of all had been to sleep in peace on that first night, knowing that in the morning they would wake not having to contend with sick stomachs knotted with nervous tension.

Bathed, cleaned and refreshed, they had descended on Paris like a miniature whirlwind, sharing drink and women with equal abandon, making every precious hour stretch into the length of a day, the Frenchmen taking an unreluctant Armstrong under their wings as they conducted him around the capital. On one occasion, they had narrowly prevented him from taking a swipe at a British brigadier

93

who, entertaining a bejewelled lady in a high-class hotel (from which they had been summarily ejected moments later, bearing trophies that included the brigadier's hat) had referred to them in a loud voice as an unruly rabble.

Closing one eye, because he was seeing three of everything, Armstrong caught a glimpse through the smoke of a figure in dark blue French Air Force uniform weaving its way towards their table, then realised that the figure wasn't weaving at all. He was, swaying from side to side in his seat.

The newcomer was Villeneuve. He grabbed a chair from an adjacent table and drew it up next to Armstrong's. He looked pale and drawn, and Armstrong suddenly realised with a feeling of guilt that his temporary commanding officer had not been enjoying a rest, as they had. Unsteadily, he reached out for a half-full bottle and filled an empty glass, pushing it towards the colonel. The latter picked it up and toyed with it, then set it down on the table untouched.

"The news is not good, my friend," he said, just loud enough for Armstrong to hear. The other pilots, engrossed in conversation with a couple of female singers who had just descended from the stage of the night club, had not yet noticed the arrival of their commander.

"I have been to a briefing session at Vincennes," Villeneuve went on. "I fear it is all over in the north. The Belgians are on the point of collapse and the British are making preparations for a major evacuation from the Channel ports. Boulogne and Calais have fallen and German tanks are pushing on towards Dunkirk, from where the British have already begun to evacuate non-combatant troops. A British armoured attack at Arras has ended in failure, although severe losses were inflicted on the enemy. The attack did not succeed because we, the French, failed to launch a simultaneous assault on the enemy's southern flank," he added bitterly.

Armstrong, feeling much more sober than he had a couple of minutes earlier, focused on Villeneuve's face.

"What now?" he asked, although in his heart he already knew the answer. His companion shrugged.

"The Germans will first of all do everything in their power to destroy the British Expeditionary Force, in my opinion. Then, once they have recovered their strength, they will launch a major offensive southward across the Somme to overwhelm the rest of France."

Villeneuve's appraisal of the Germans' intentions was shrewd, but he was wrong on one point. The British counter-attack at Arras against General Rommel's 7th *Panzer* Division had not failed because of any lack of co-operation on the part of the French. Initially, the British Matilda tanks had played havoc with the enemy's motor transport, sending much of it up in flames with tracer ammunition. The enemy anti-tank gunners, after firing a few rounds, had abandoned their weapons and bolted, even though the Matildas were still six to eight hundred yards from them; some surrendered, while others lay on the ground and played dead. None of the Matildas were penetrated by the German anti-tank shot, and none were destroyed by high explosive artillery shells. One Matilda took fourteen direct hits from 37-mm guns, and other than gouging out bits of armour, the shells did no damage.

In fact, the British thrust was only halted when it came up against 88-mm anti-aircraft guns, hastily converted to anti-tank weapons on Rommel's orders and firing over open sights. Not even the Matildas' thickness of armour could withstand their high-velocity shells, and the attack eventually ground to a halt just as it was about to complete a semi-circle around Arras. The British casualty list was fairly heavy, the supporting infantry having been subjected to air attack, but the losses of the 7th *Panzer* Division were heavier still: 89 killed, 116 wounded, and 173 missing. Added to this the British took 400 prisoners, mostly from the SS *Totenkopf* Division, whose troops had shown signs of panic; which meant that on this one day alone, Rommel's division suffered four times the losses it had sustained during the breakthrough across the Meuse. Small wonder that the German general recorded in his diary that he had been confronted by no fewer than five divisions with hundreds of tanks; in reality, about seventy-five Matildas had been involved.

Armstrong, with his index finger, was idly playing with a small pool of wine that had been spilt on the table top. Without realising it, he had turned the pool into Paris, and was drawing thin defensive lines around it, in burgundy-coloured concentric circles. Almost as though he had read the Englishman's mind, Villeneuve said:

"Every fighter group that can be spared is being assembled for the defence of the capital. We fear that the Germans will launch a major air attack on Paris in the hope of compelling us to surrender. Just imagine, all our beautiful buildings, all our heritage, destroyed . . ." His voice trailed away and he stared into the tobacco smoke, stricken by the thought.

Armstrong was also staring into the smoke, but for a different reason. Two men had just come into the bar and were trying to order drinks above the general hubbub. Armstrong narrowed his eyes, trying to make out the features of the taller of the two, who wore the insignia of a French Air Force *commandant* – the equivalent of a squadron leader in the RAF. A moment later, he knew that he was right. It was Stanislaw Kalinski.

Making his excuses to Villeneuve, he got up somewhat unsteadily and pushed his way through the throng. The Polish officer, for such he was, did not notice Armstrong's approach. The latter waited until Kalinski had caught a waitresses's eye and then coughed politely.

"Mine's a cognac," he said.

Kalinski swung round and his mouth dropped open as he recognised the RAF pilot. Drink forgotten, he seized a suddenly embarrassed Armstrong in a bear hug, slapping him on the back, then released him and addressed his companion in a torrent of Polish. The other Pole nodded solemnly as Kalinski described, in a few sentences, the

96

adventures he and Armstrong had shared in Norway just a few weeks earlier. Kalinski had been there as a member of the French Expeditionary Force, flying an observation aircraft, and Armstrong had acted as his gunner after his own photo-recce Spitfire had been destroyed in an air attack on a frozen lake near Aandalsnes. Both had got out of Norway by the skin of their teeth, one step ahead of the advancing Germans.

Kalinski paused in mid-sentence, leaving his fellow officer looking somewhat bewildered, and turned to Armstrong, seizing his arm. "But – please forgive my bad manners, my friend. Let me introduce you to someone who has been a comrade in arms since the start of this war. Flight Lieutenant Kenneth Armstrong – Captain Jan Rabanowski. We were in the same fighter squadron in Poland; together we fought the Germans, and together we escaped."

Rabanowski clicked his heels and bowed slightly, shaking Armstrong's hand. Armstrong, suddenly overcome by a fit of drink-induced mirth, wondered how he managed to accomplish all three manoeuvres at the same time. Rabanowski, friendly but rather reticent, spoke no English but was able to converse in French.

Armstrong and Kalinski were equally amazed to meet up with one another in Paris. The Pole acquired a round of drinks and the three of them found a corner, where Armstrong told him how he came to be there. Kalinski, in turn, explained that after getting back to France after the ill-starred first Norwegian expedition, he had been given the task of forming a fighter squadron made up entirely of Polish personnel, who at that time were scattered all over the country with various French units after having got out of German-occupied Poland.

"As you may imagine, I jumped at the chance," Kalinski said. "Off I went, clutching my new orders, to Lyon-Bron, where the nucleus of an outfit called the *École de Chasse et d'Instruction Polonaise* – the Polish Fighter Instruction School – had already been formed. Pilots and mechanics, all of them Polish, were gradually being posted in, and the school had twenty-five fighters – Morane 406s, most of them in pretty good condition – so I was quite happy. Training proceeded as per schedule, the pilots converted to the Morane without any trouble – in fact, some of them, like Jan here, had flown it already with French squadrons and had seen combat."

He paused to light a cigarette, adding a stream of smoke to the general fog in the room before continuing. "We were just about to be declared operational when the blow fell. Our nice Moranes were to be allocated to another unit, and we were to go to war flying Caudron 714s."

"Never heard of 'em," Armstrong said. Kalinski gave a wry smile.

"An interesting little beast, the Caudron. It has its good points and its bad – mostly bad. It performance is inferior to the Morane's on most counts, and a long way below the Me 109's. The French Government ordered it, I believe, because it was simple and cheap to build. The first aircraft were delivered last January, and there were plans to send them to Finland, manned by Polish volunteers – of whom I was one – to fight the Russians. We wouldn't have minded that," he added grimly.

"Anyway," he went on, "all that came to nothing when the Finns and the Russians signed their armistice last March. So off I went to Norway, as you know. To cut a long story short, I am now the rather less than enthusiastic commander of a squadron called GC I/146. We have fifteen Caudrons and we are based at Dreux, south-west of Paris. We are moving up to Le Bourget in the morning."

"That's where we are," Armstrong told him. "We were at Anglure, then we were deployed to Le Bourget for a special mission. Afterwards, we were told to stay there. I was supposed to rejoin the RAF ages ago, but it looks as though I'm stuck with the French for the duration."

Suddenly, he realised that he had forgotten all about Villeneuve and the other French pilots. He looked around at the place where they had been sitting, and saw that they were gone; presumably, in the confusion of the crowded bar, they must have thought that he had left before them.

He had a few more drinks with the two Poles and then decided that it was time to pack his bags and return to Le Bourget to try to catch a few hours' sleep before facing whatever the next day might bring. Bidding his companions farewell, he returned to his hotel, a couple of streets away, to find that the French pilots had checked out a while earlier. They had been looking for him, he was told. His bill had been settled by the colonel.

He packed his bag and went out into the night, locating a taxi without difficulty. Despite the doom that was about to descend upon it, the nightlife of Paris was in full swing, and the rush to obtain cabs had not yet begun.

As the taxi picked its way through the imperfect blackout, Armstrong, feeling suddenly sick and dizzy from the effects of too much beer and tobacco, prayed that the German bombers would give the battered fighter squadrons at least a day's respite before they descended on the French capital.

His prayer was answered. For the time being, the bombers were busy elsewhere.

Chapter Eight

THE ROAD TO DUNKIRK: SOLDIERS' TALES

Along the narrow roads, strafed and dive-bombed, tortured by thirst and the pangs of hunger, the khaki columns streamed back towards Dunkirk. Ahead of them, trailing its sombre cloak across the May sky by day and providing a lurid beacon by night, was the funeral pyre of the town; behind them the rumble of battle as the rearguard actions continued; and on all sides reeking debris and corpses.

Despite the confusion, despite the exhaustion, despite the agony of blistered, lacerated feet and the burden of equipment that weighed like lead, despite the uncertainty and fear, most units – whether of company strength or split up into small parties – maintained a high degree of cohesion and discipline. And through the haze of fatigue, the nightmare of that march back to the salvation of the English Channel would etch itself indelibly into the minds of many.

The sun shines; the sky is a cloudless blue. The *Luftwaffe* is everywhere, smashing everything that moves. We are surrounded by field guns, and we share with the gunners ninety minutes of dive-bombing *Stukas*: the terror weapon. Helpless, we cower in the ditches and pray. Hedge-hopping fighters machine gun us – spurts of dust in the road – whoosh of flame and smoke from stricken vehicles. Noise. Smoke. Flame. Why are we here? How did we reach this place? We know that the *Boche* has cut our routes to the south and west and is assaulting also from the north and east, but we do not accept these facts because we do not want to accept them. As a unit we are now valueless except as individuals with rifles – any time now we may find a desperate use for these. The day wears slowly on; we wait for we know not what. We are very frightened.

Then, at 1700 hours, orders! Smash all equipment, burn all secret documents. Make for the coast and report to the Navy! Never in British history has that phrase seemed so important. To our young ears it means salvation – if only we can make the coast. We set off in the warm, sunny afternoon back to Armentières, through Comines and on to Messines Ridge, where we are held up by a squadron of Belgian cavalry. Incredible to see horse soldiers! On along the hot, dusty road towards Ypres, turning off for Poperinghe.

We pushed on, throwing all wrecked instruments, clothing, the ashes of documents, gas cylinders, anything that could be abandoned, into the roadside ditches. On across the 1914–18 battlefields into which our fathers had poured their blood, holding on against the same enemy; bitter thoughts. Shortly before midnight we arrived in Hoogstade, where all small vehicles were wrecked and abandoned and we devoured our last scraps of food. After an hour or so we all crammed into the larger vehicles and set off through the night for Bulscamp. It was a night of fatigue and frustration, with tired drivers cursing and each of us wrapped in his own private cocoon of fear, doubt, and thoughts of home.

We reached Bulscamp late in the morning and were issued with messy coloured water which the cooks called tea. Now the ordeal really began, for we were ordered to split up into parties of twenty-five and make a forced march to Teteghem, east of Dunkirk. Laden with small arms, ammunition and the kit of some officer – severe doubts cast on his parentage – our party set out for the sea.

101

There was little doubt about the point we were making for; away to the north-east rose a vast plume of smoke.

Our leader was an attached officer of the French Military Mission, armed with a map torn from a school atlas. This gentleman succeeded twice in leading us astray, but on both occasions units of the RAOC and RASC turned us back from the direction in which we were heading, which would have brought us into contact with the enemy, and set us on the right road. A captain of the RASC was deeply suspicious and suggested that we took steps to eliminate him, this being no time for squeamishness. We managed to ditch him further along the road.

At Teteghem, we were allowed thirty minutes' rest and some food – two 12-ounce tins of bully beef between the twenty-five of us, plus two hardtack biscuits per man. On these scant provisions, exhausted in mind and body, torn between despair and hope, we renewed our march to the outskirts of Dunkirk and made our way through the rubble to the sand dunes beyond. Against the darkening sky the flames of the burning town were reflected in the sullen canals and waterways, silhouetting other marching groups.

We passed a battery of destroyed anti-aircraft guns, their barrels split open and curled back like sticks of celery. Over everything hung the towering pall of black smoke from the burning oil tanks, stretching across the western horizon. Forward we stumbled, a cursing, motley crew, calling upon our ebbing physical and mental strength to push one foot in front of the other, some of us with boots that squelched blood. So we came to the dunes, where we halted, to fall and sleep in the sand and the coarse grass.

– An RAF airman, a member of ground crew,
caught up in the retreat to Dunkirk;
28 May, 1940

In the early hours the section I was in was ordered back to a farmhouse on a small hill. Things were rather quiet at first, but about 3 am we came under shellfire that grew more intense as time went by, and at dawn the enemy were within small-arms range. Soon afterwards we were told to go down to the forward positions to help strengthen the line. As we left the farmhouse the enemy started belting us with the most accurate mortar fire I have ever seen. There were six of us, and the bombs were actually falling among us as we ran. It was impossible to take more than one or two strides before a fresh bomb sent us face down in the dirt. I saw one man with his hand sliced clean off. They mortared us all the way down the slope until we reached the breastworks at the bottom; they had been built during the 1914–18 war and formed our main defences. Our arrival was greeted by an enemy observation plane, which dropped a smoke marker almost on our heads – the signal for more mortar fire.

Not long afterwards a stream of chaps came along from B Company, or what was left of them; they said that the Germans had overrun No. 1 Platoon and that now there was nothing to prevent the breaking through *en masse*. Our officers, Captain Rylands and Lieutenant Partridge, conferred and decided to pull us out to higher ground, as we had no chance of holding our present positions.

As we started to move out the Germans let go with everything they had – artillery, mortars, Spandaus. The concentration of fire was terrific. The only way to reach the high ground was through a group of cottages straddling the road a couple of hundred yards away; the fields around were lined with fine-mesh wire fences and we would have been picked off easily as we tried to get over them. So we doubled off down the road, about two hundred of us I suppose, all making for one house in particular which seemed to have a large garden; we intended to work our way through it from front to rear.

Just as we reached the house down came the mortar bombs, right in among us. I was well to the rear, and as I crept closer I could see a group of men struggling to get through the garden gate. Smoke and flames were everywhere and the ground shuddered with explosions. I looked up again, and suddenly it seemed that everyone else had gone and that I was alone; a terrifying feeling. Then, as I crawled nearer the gate, I saw a man lying in a pool of water. He had been badly hit in the back. I got him out of the water and laid him by the side of the road. He didn't want me to leave him and clung to me as hard as he could. There was nothing I could do, and my fear of being taken prisoner was strong. In the end, muttering something about going to get help, I left the poor chap and threw myself under cover on the other side of the road.

I inched along on this side until I was opposite the garden gate, then dashed across the road again and through into the garden. There was a fearful mess all around the gate; men had been killed ten times over, their bodies ripped apart by the mortar bombs. I went into the garden; there wasn't a soul in sight and I had no idea where they had gone, so I thought I would just keep going in a straight line and hope for the best.

After going a short way I came upon a soldier who was terribly wounded in the waist area. The legs of his trousers were soaked in blood; there wasn't a patch of khaki to be seen. I asked him which way the others had gone; he showed me and off I went. Away on the hill ahead I could see a lot of smoke and shellbursts, and I guessed that was where our chaps would be. A few moments later I spotted a line of lorries, looking just like toys as they moved along the road that wound up the hillside. A terrible panic seized me; I thought Christ, they're going off without me, and I started to run. Although I was pretty well exhausted the running caused me no effort at all. It seemed as though my legs didn't belong to me.

After a while I staggered into a little hamlet near the foot of the hill, where to my relief I came across two of my mates, Tom Calow and Johnny Kemble. There was a fearful barrage in progress; it was absolutely pouring with mortar bombs and those terrible shrapnel shells. Compared with that the bullets didn't amount to much really; nobody took much notice of them.

We made our way along a ditch to a farm where Company HQ had been set up. Most of the chaps who were left had assembled there. We were reformed to make a counter-attack. There didn't seem to be much point in it really, but we set off just the same, advancing down to the valley until we came out on to a track where we took cover among some trees. My friend Tom had gone to the top of the hill with Lieutenant 'Ginger' Partridge; sometime later he came running back with two bullets in his side. He was a little tough sort of kid, but he was sweating quite a bit and I advised him to take off his equipment and make his way back to HQ before he became too weak. He pushed his way into a hayfield and that was the last I ever saw of him.

We were unable to continue the advance, for the enemy had gained some high ground on either side and we were caught in a crossfire. There was no alternative but to pull out. Our advance had brought us down to where the soldier with the bloodstained trousers lay, and we brought him out with us. Our only avenue of escape lay along a ditch that bordered the track. It was broken at intervals by gateways where other tracks led into the fields on either side. The leading group of men reached the first of these openings, raised themselves out of the ditch and started to make their way across. It looked as though they were going to make it when suddenly the Spandaus opened up and cut them to ribbons.

105

I could see men still trying to run across among all that murderous fire, but I stayed where I was until things quietened down a bit and then I crawled over, sheltering behind the bodies of the poor devils who lay in the gateway. I got back into the ditch, which was full of crawling men. It was very shallow and the Spandaus were pecking away at us all the time; as soon as you raised your head you drew a burst of fire, and every time a man was hit in front of you, you had to crawl over the top of him, which made you still more vulnerable. There were about six gateways, with tracks traversing the ditch, and every time you came to one you had to get up and take a flying leap to the other side. Every opening had those hellish machine-guns trained on it. When it came to my turn I made a terrific leap, aiming to land a few yards along the ditch; land short, and the odds were that you would come down on top of someone, in which case the machine-guns would have you.

I crawled on up the ditch, together with the other survivors. Suddenly, I was almost sick. In front if my face lay a man's liver, still steaming. I eased myself over it carefully and went on. It must have taken us three hours to crawl along that ditch. In the end I reached the last gateway, and prepared to make my usual flying leap. Perhaps I was over-confident; perhaps I didn't move fast enough. At any rate, as I jumped a Spandau got me in the leg. I landed heavily, swearing hard – not so much because of the pain, but because I thought my leg was broken. I found that I could still move it, however, so things didn't seem quite so bad.

Those of us that were left eventually got back to the farm and Lieutenant Partridge led us back to our transport, which was waiting some way further back. The enemy shellfire was not so intense now, because it was dusk and the valley was filled with drifting smoke from the barrage they had been putting up all day. It helped to screen us from the enemy guns.

We boarded the lorries and went away into the night. Lots of times, as we drove on, we heard the cries of wounded men, begging us to stop. But there was no stopping; nobody was really interested in the wounded. It was the fit men who mattered now. And so, filthy, exhausted and bloodstained, we made our way back towards Furnes on the Dunkirk perimeter.

We hadn't been there long when an officer came along and crawled into the lorry, wanting to know how many men there were with rifles. Nobody answered him. 'Come on,' he said, 'Senior NCOs!' Still nobody moved. He got a torch and shone it into the face of a sergeant, then on the face of each man in turn. After a long pause he nodded, as though in sympathy, and left. It wasn't cowardice on their part, when they didn't answer; it was just the fact that human beings can have just about enough. If you are hungry, exhausted and shell-shocked you just don't want any more.

That was where I left them, and that was where they made their last stand.

I went down to the hospital at La Panne, with the huge Red Cross flag flying over it. Until now I had never really believed all the stories about Dunkirk, and evacuation; but now that I saw the sea I began to have an inkling that they might be true after all . . .

– A soldier of the 4th Battalion,
the Royal Berkshire Regiment,
29 May 1940

It was dark when we reached the sandhills and we were very tired. The day before, or it might have been the day before that, guncotton and detonators had been issued with orders to blow up the guns. Since then the purpose of our existence had changed. We were no longer a fighting force but simply a unit moving back towards the coast.

Behind the sandhills lay the sea, and beyond the sea – England. This seemed incredible and wholly beyond one's comprehension, but lack of sleep dulls the senses and blunts the ability to comprehend. We lay down where we stood and slept where we lay down; I found I was on the edge of a trench and dropped into it. I awoke in a grey still dawn to the sound of a voice reciting French. Looking over the lip of the trench I saw a French burial party at work a few yards away and realised my trench was a grave. I got out and walked away.

An hour later the order came for us to move down to the beach, and we made our way over the sand hills. It was now quite light, and as we came to the edge of the dunes we saw the beach spread out before us, stretching away on either side. As far as we could see it was black with men. They were in groups, in broken lines and circles; sitting, lying and standing – all of them waiting. Just in front of us someone had tried to build a jetty of lorries. They were placed head to tail, two abreast, and stretched out into the sea. A few men were clambering along them, but otherwise no one seemed to be interested.

We sat down in the sand and waited. Offshore were ships and boats of various shapes and sizes from destroyers downwards; some were moving and others were apparently at anchor. By this time the sun had risen and revealed the clear blue sky of an early summer morning, and with the sun came the *Stukas*. They approached from behind us, spread out according to their fancy and proceeded to bomb what they liked . . .

– An officer of the 68th
Field Battery, Royal
Artillery, 30 May 1940

We arrived off the beaches and were detailed to proceed to La Panne, bringing off as many soldiers as possible. The scene on the beaches at La Panne at this time was very depressing, with dark groups of soldiers huddled together in small parties. Through the twilight we could see the oil tanks burning in the distance, and occasional flashes of gunfire lit up the horizon. The boats were lowered, each manned by one sailor; they were towed to the beach by a motor launch and filled to capacity, the troops manning the oars and pulling back to the ship.

This process went on all night. Just before dawn a boatload of wounded came in; as soon as the men were taken aboard one of them, an officer of the Durham Light Infantry, came up to our first lieutenant and asked to be put back ashore, as there were more wounded to be looked after. 'Jimmy' told him that he was very sorry; the ship had taken on her full quota, with every inch of space occupied above and below, and the sooner she could unload her troops in England the sooner she would be back.

The army officer pleaded, but to no avail. Suddenly, he turned and wandered away, past the 12-pounder which I was manning. He looked all in and utterly dejected. Then, from around the stern, came the putt-putt of a motor boat. The officer hailed it; it came quietly round the stern and he took a flying leap into it from the afterdeck. The boat disappeared into the night and I never saw him again. As he went I looked at the beach, at the burning oil tanks and the flashing of the guns; and I knew that I would not have had the courage to do what he did that night . . .

– A Royal Navy gunner
on the fleet minesweeper HMS *Dundalk*, 31 May 1940

And so, in destroyers, minesweepers, cross-Channel ferries, trawlers, stream packets and an armada of small civilian craft manned by gallant volunteers, the thousands came back from Dunkirk and its neighbouring beaches. Overhead, the Spitfire and Hurricane squadrons of RAF Fighter Command, often unseen by the haggard men far below, fought it out with the *Luftwaffe*. But Fighter Command's sternest test was yet to come, over the harvest fields of southern England.

So long as the English tongue survives, the word Dunkirk will be spoken with reverence. For in that harbour, in such a hell as never blazed on earth before, at the end of a lost battle, the rags and blemishes that have hidden the soul of Democracy fell away. There, beaten but unconquered in shining splendour she faced the enemy. This shining thing in the souls of free men Hitler cannot command or attain or conquer . . . It is the greatest tradition of Democracy. It is the future. It is Victory.

– The *New York Times*,
1 June 1940

Chapter Nine

One hundred and twenty miles to the south of the embattled beaches of Dunkirk, the Allied fighter pilots – French, Poles, Czechs, a handful of Belgians and at least one Briton – waited for the expected onslaught on Paris. For a while it seemed that Providence was on their side, for during the first two days of June fog and drizzle shrouded almost the whole of France and the Low Countries. It brought a respite from the *Luftwaffe*'s ceaseless attacks on the ships that were taking the last troops from Dunkirk: men of General Fournel de la Laurencie's French III Corps, who had gallantly held the perimeter, and who now scooped up handfuls of French earth, to be stored reverently in pockets, wallets and handkerchiefs as they filed down to the waiting boats, to remind them of their homeland until the day – and only God knew when that would be – when they would stand on the soil of France again; and it brought relief for the battered French fighter squadrons that were now preparing to defend Paris to the last aircraft and last pilot, if need be.

The bad weather cleared in the early hours of 3 June, and the fighter pilots were called to readiness at dawn. The morning was hot and oppressive, with a hint of thunder in the air. Some of the pilots had started the day wearing their flying overalls; by noon, they were in their shirt sleeves. Armstrong was one of them.

It came as pure relief when, at 1300, the alarm finally sounded. Three massive formations of enemy bombers, with a strong fighter escort, had been sighted over Reims, Saint

111

Quentin and Cambrai. No order to take off was received as yet – it was the task of the fighter squadrons forming the outer defensive screen to engage the enemy first – but faces became grim as reports of the size of the enemy raid began to trickle in. In all, 500 enemy aircraft were heading for Paris. The French fighters were outnumbered five to one.

Armstrong and his fellow pilots sat impatiently in their cockpits, motors ticking over, anxiously watching the needles of their engine temperature gauges climbing remorselessly towards the red zone, waiting for the order to go. Over their radios, which were tuned to a common fighter frequency, they could hear sounds of the battle that was beginning to develop on the northern approaches to the capital.

The progress of the *Luftwaffe* formations was being reported by the crews of some Potez 631s, who shadowed them at a discreet distance and provided a running commentary on the enemy's course, altitude and so on. This information, together with the order for the fighters to take off, was supposed to be retransmitted to the fighter bases via a radio station that had been set up in the Eiffel Tower, but it was being heavily jammed by the enemy and the messages were so garbled and distorted that they were useless.

In any case, the reports from the Potez ceased abruptly when the Messerschmitts pounced and shot them out of the sky, one after the other.

By 1310, Colonel Villeneuve had had enough. Over the radio, he ordered his group to take off. As they began to taxi, Armstrong saw that Kalinski was of like mind; the angular little Caudron fighters, bearing the red-and-white checkerboard insignia of Poland on their wings, were also starting to move.

Whatever the outcome, Armstrong told himself, there was certain to be one hell of a free-for-all over Paris this afternoon.

They took off in their two flights of three, all that was

left of them, Villeneueve leading one and Armstrong the other, and climbed hard over the sprawl of Paris. Armstrong looked across in turn at each of his wingmen, two sergeants named Duval and Morel, and waved reassuringly at them. They knew what they must do in the coming battle; all of them did. With the odds stacked against them, there was no room for textbook tactics.

The French reporting system, without the benefit of radio direction finding, was primitive and ineffectual. RAF fighter squadrons in England, alerted by the probing rays sent out by the RDF masts on the south coast, would have been 'mixing it' with the enemy by now. The French, on the other hand, relied on an antiquated telephone network to report the progress of approaching aircraft, or on visual observation from the air.

Still, Armstrong thought with awe and not a little trepidation, it would be hard to miss *that* lot. At 19,000 feet, strung out across the sky over the suburbs of Paris, was the biggest armada of aircraft he had ever seen. The sky was black with them. They were flying in wedges, like skeins of geese, sliding between towering thunderclouds. And above them, silvery crosses in the sunlight, their guardian Messerschmitt formations crossed over one another's path in a steady tactical rhythm, their pilots watchful.

Villeneuve's dry, calm voice came over the R/T, its tone setting nerves at ease for the moment.

"Doubtless you can see the enemy," he said. "Do not fight amongst yourselves over which targets to choose. There are plenty. Line abreast, attack! Tally Ho!"

Armstrong laughed out loud in the cockpit. The 'tally ho' was a cry Villeneuve had enthusiastically borrowed from the RAF pilot; the French did not seem to have an equivalent.

The fighter pilots spread out, a couple of hundred yards between each aircraft, each picking a target as the two formations closed with one another at something like 500 miles per hour. It was a closing speed that left very little margin for error.

Throwing a quick glance to either side to make sure that his two wingmen were in position, Armstrong selected a flight of Heinkels that was flying a little lower than the rest and put his Hawk into a shallow dive, building up speed. Concentrating on the centre bomber of the enemy flight, he gripped the control column with both hands, bracing his whole body as the Heinkel's wingspan expanded rapidly in his gunsight. Smoky tendrils speared out from the Heinkel's nose, reaching towards him. They dropped away beneath the Hawk as the German gunner, doubtless rattled by the fighter bearing down on him head-on, missed his target.

Armstrong squeezed the triggers and the image of the Heinkel shivered in his windscreen. There was time only for a two-second burst of fire before he was compelled to shove the stick forward hard to avoid the looming bulk of the bomber. His guts rose into his chest as the Hawk plummeted down, missing the Heinkel's underside by feet.

He pulled back on the stick again, the force of gravity pushing him down in his seat as he zoomed up under a second formation of bombers, loosing off a burst at one of them as he hurtled past, with no visible result. The impetus of his zoom-climb carried him up a couple of thousand feet and he stall-turned the fighter, coming down astern of the bombers. Sinister black eggs were tumbling from their bellies now as they released their bomb loads; the first wave was already turning away as the bombs fell towards factories and power stations, and inevitably the houses that clustered around them, in the Parisian suburbs. Smoke trails, arrowing down towards the haze below, marked the last plunge of two aircraft; whether they were German or French it was impossible to tell.

Armstrong came down hard on the tail of a Heinkel on the lefthand side of the rearmost formation and, bracing every fibre of his body again, held the Hawk steady as he closed in, ignoring the fire that came at him from the bomber's dorsal gun position. He knew that with the Hawk's poor armament, the only real chance of success was to get in really close, to punch hard with a couple of well-aimed bursts, inflicting the maximum possible damage, before quickly getting out of danger.

The Heinkel suddenly went into a steep turn to the left. Armstrong followed it, firing a burst into its starboard engine. The effect was startling. Large fragments broke away, whirling back in the slipstream. The Heinkel skidded violently out of its turn and a cloud of white smoke burst from the stricken engine. The bomber's starboard undercarriage leg dropped from its raised position in the engine nacelle and hung in the slipstream. The smoke thickened, shot with flame now, and the Heinkel went into a spiral dive. Armstrong pulled up above it and steep-turned, looking down on the bomber's death agony. It left a corkscrew of smoke in the sky as it spiralled down towards the haze that was growing thicker over Paris with every passing minute. Two black dots tumbled from it, trailing bright yellow streamers that blossomed into parachutes. They drifted down behind the bomber as the haze enveloped it.

Armstrong weaved his fighter from side to side, looking round. Only now did he become conscious that the radio was filled with chatter. Drifting clouds of spent anti-aircraft bursts filled the sky, adding to the murk hanging like a veil over the French capital; through it, the broad ribbon of the Seine shone dully.

Armstrong was suddenly frightened. He had been quite calm while engaging the enemy, and surprisingly had experienced no elation at shooting down the Heinkel. Now, as though a giant hand had wiped the sky clear, it was suddenly empty of aircraft. He was isolated, and felt utterly alone and exposed. He found himself shivering in the cockpit. It was as though some sixth sense were prodding at his nervous system. A sixth sense. Frantically, he looked behind.

Jesus! Two aircraft were sitting on his tail, still several hundred yards away but closing rapidly. Short, square-cut wings. Messerschmitt 109s.

Armstrong knew instinctively that if he tried to turn and face them head-on at this range one of them would almost certainly nail him as he turned. The 109s were well spaced out, with a quarter of a mile between them, and were in a position to box him in without difficulty. His only hope was to try to shake them off in the thickening haze, which was becoming really dense a few thousand feet below.

He put the Hawk into a dive and opened the throttle wide, his heart in his mouth. A glance in his rear-view mirror showed that the 109s were following and keeping pace with him. One of the enemy fighters had drawn some distance ahead of its companion. Yellow flashes of gunfire twinkled on its nose.

There was a hollow thud somewhere in the Hawk's fuselage, followed instantly by a metallic clatter of shrapnel on the armour plating behind Armstrong's seat. He risked a glance to the rear again, and saw with relief that the outlines of the pursuing fighters were becoming blurred. They must be having real difficulty in seeing him now.

Armstrong held the fighter in its drive, knowing that he still had about 8,000 feet of height in hand before he made a hole in the middle of Paris. At 4,000 feet he gently began to pull back on the stick, using both hands because the controls were stiff with the speed of the dive and praying that nothing vital had been damaged by the Messerschmitt's fire. The Hawk shuddered but responded magnificently.

Armstrong maintained the backward pressure and pulled the fighter up into the beginning of a loop, hoping that the German fighter pilots had logical Teutonic minds. They would not be expecting him to do that. The logical thing to do in his circumstances would be to level out just above the rooftops of Paris and head flat out for home, hoping the enemy fighters would be drawn into the flak barrage. Instead, Armstrong half-rolled off the top of the loop and headed in the opposite direction, climbing at full throttle. A couple of minutes later he popped out of the layer of haze and drifting smoke, which the wind at altitude had flattened out until it was like the surface of a lake, with stirred-up whorls and eddies breaking it up here and there.

He was just in time to see the two Messerschmitts turning towards the north, half a mile away, flying almost wingtip to wingtip just above the hazy layer. They were not hurrying, and he quickly realised that their pilots had not spotted him. Every nerve tense, Armstrong stalked them, gradually overhauling them. Odd buffeting noises were coming from somewhere in the rear of the Hawk, but he did his best to ignore them.

He was within two hundred yards of the left-hand Messerschmitt. It went into a gentle turn to the right, following its leader; it was now some distance behind the other aircraft. Its pilot must surely see him. Hang on, he told himself. Closer, closer still. At less than a hundred yards he opened fire.

The grey outline of the Messerschmitt wobbled and the shining arc of its propeller broke up, its blades windmilling. Bullet strikes danced and sparkled along the 109's length from nose to wingtip. Dense white smoke belched back over its wings and it started to go down.

The cockpit canopy flew off and a moment later the dark shape of the pilot emerged, arms and legs spreadeagled, seemingly attached to the falling aircraft. Then the airflow caught him and he fell clear, disappearing under Armstrong's wing, falling towards the city below.

Armstrong did not look to see whether the German's parachute had opened. He went after the leading 109, which was flying steadily on, its pilot apparently unaware of what had happened. Armstrong suddenly realised that it was gaining on him, and a quick look at his instruments told him that his fuel state was dangerously low. He also knew that he must be almost out of ammunition. Reluctantly he let the German go and turned away, descending through the haze to get his bearings. A few minutes later he located Le Bourget and circled the airfield before making his approach to land.

The bombers had been there. There were craters everywhere, the hangars were in ruins and the airfield was littered with wrecked aircraft, mostly trainers and transports which had not been involved in the fighting. Armstrong touched down on a patch of undamaged earth and taxied in, threading his way between the craters to a spot near one of the hangars where he could see a couple more Hawks. One of them was Villeneuve's; the other belonged to his wingman, Duval.

The rest of the group, and most of the Polish Caudrons, were scattered on airfields all over the Paris region. Those that had survived.

Duval came to meet him as he climbed from the cockpit and dropped off the wing, flexing his arms and legs. The sergeant's face was drawn.

"Where's Morel?" Armstrong queried anxiously.

"I'm afraid he's gone, sir," Duval said quietly. "I saw him collide head-on with a Heinkel. There was no chance that he might have got out."

"Poor devil." Armstrong did not know what else to say; he was aware that Duval and Morel had been close friends. He fished in his tunic pocket for his pipe, which he had filled before take-off, and lit it, exhaling a cloud of pungent French *Jean Bart* tobacco. "What's happened to the colonel?"

"He is in the flight hut, sir, trying to find out what has become of the other pilots. He shot down two bombers. I also got one, by the way. A Dornier. Did you have any luck?"

Armstrong smiled and clapped the NCO on the shoulder. "Well done!" he said warmly, knowing that it was Duval's first victory. "Yes, I got a couple too, a Heinkel and a 109. We would have knocked down more of them, too, if only we had received orders to take off in time. And perhaps poor Morel would still have been with us."

Duval nodded, reddening, and turned away to hide the emotions that had clearly welled up inside him. Armstrong patted his shoulder again and left him to seek out Villeneuve. He found the colonel where Duval had said he would be, sitting beside a telephone. Villeneuve's face brightened as Armstrong came in.

"You are like the cat with its nine lives, my friend. I was certain that this time, you had used them all up." He gestured towards a chair and leaned back in his own, lighting a cigarette. "You know we have lost Sergeant Morel?" Armstrong nodded. "A great pity," Villeneuve said. "A good pilot, and one with much potential. He failed to break off his attack in time. A split second of misjudgement, and *pouf* – gone. Extinguished like the flame of this match."

"What about the others?" Armstrong asked.

"Fortunately, all safe. They either called up over the radio to say that they were landing elsewhere, or telephoned straight away. They know how I concern myself about them," he added, smiling.

The smile did nothing to hide the weariness on Villeneuve's face. He had aged ten years in less than a month.

"Have you heard anything of the Poles?" Armstrong wanted to know. Villeneuve nodded. "Ah, yes, the Poles. They took a look at the damage here and went off to land at Dreux and Brétigny. Very wise. Your friend Kalinski telephoned to say that they destroyed two Messerschmitt 109s for no loss to themselves. I told him to keep his aircraft and pilots where they were. It is possible that we may have to evacuate Le Bourget shortly."

As the afternoon wore on, and reports of the day's fighting came in, it became apparent that the Le Bourget squadrons had been lucky, possibly because the few fighter groups that had received the order to take off had absorbed the first shock of the enemy raid on Paris, which the Germans had code-named Operation Paula.

Among the units that had received the alert was *Groupe de Chasse* I/III, whose seventeen Dewoitine D.520s had been among the first to take off from their airfield at Meaux, a few miles from the capital. As they attacked a formation of enemy bombers, the French pilots were heavily engaged by the enemy fighter escort, and were soon fighting for their lives. In the space of five minutes two of them were shot down and killed and three more wounded, in return for which they could claim only one Me 109 destroyed and three bombers damaged.

Nevertheless, the arrival of the D.520s had averted another tragedy. A few minutes ahead of them, nine Morane 406s had taken off from Coulommiers with a formation of bombers already in sight. The fighter pilots made a head-on attack in the course of which they destroyed a Junkers 88 and an Me 109, but when they went after the formation for a second attack they found that their weary Moranes could not match the bombers' speed. Then the Messerschmitts were upon them, and all the Morane pilots could do was to keep turning as tightly as possible and wait for an opportunity to disengage. It came when the German fighters broke off to deal with I/III's D.520s.

Another Morane 406 unit was not so lucky. At 1315 a wave of Dornier 17s swept at low altitude over its airfield at Plessis, followed a few seconds later by another wave bombing from medium level. The four Moranes on readiness were knocked out even before they had begun to taxi; four more managed to take off among the exploding bombs and exchange a few ineffectual bursts of fire with a flight of Messerschmitts that raced across the field on a strafing run, but the Messerschmitts vanished in the haze and the Moranes, with no hope of catching them, landed again on their cratered base.

Everywhere, it was the same story of disaster. At 1320, while Villeneuve and the Poles were fighting over Paris, twenty-two Marcel Bloch MB 152 radial-engined fighters took off in the face of a wave of approaching bombers and climbed furiously to meet them in two waves, one of fourteen and one of eight, trying to manoeuvre into a suitable position to attack. But the German fighters were everywhere. Fifteen Me 109s trapped a flight of Blochs and shot all three of them down in as many minutes; only one pilot managed to bale out, badly burned. Two more MB 152s went down in flames shortly afterwards, destroyed in turn after shooting down an Me 109 near Senlis. Then the Messerschmitts pounced on the second wave of climbing fighters and destroyed three of them; again, only one pilot succeeded in baling out.

At about the same time a third Bloch group took off from Bretigny. The pilots had not even had time to strap themselves in. Now, hanging on their propellers, the nine fighters climbed flat out towards the wave of bombers and Messerschmitts strung out across the sky 12,000 feet higher up. Still climbing, they attacked a formation of thirty Heinkel bombers and shot down two of them before the German fighter escort intervened. One MB 152 pilot baled out of his blazing aircraft and two more had to make forced landings.

On the southern outskirts of Paris, a dozen Moranes tangled with a formation of bombers after taking off from their base in ones and twos and climbing through a terrific barrage of French anti-aircraft fire. They destroyed a Heinkel and three Me 110s, but three French pilots were shot down and killed.

At 1340, twenty-one Curtiss Hawks of GC I/5 took off from Saint-Dizier and quickly located a formation of Dornier 17s, heading north-east. The *Groupe* was just positioning itself for a stern attack when it was heavily engaged by fifty Me 109s and 110s. During a hectic fifteen-minute dogfight the French pilots destroyed one Do 17, two Me 109s and two Me 110s for the loss of one of their own number. A second Hawk pilot, wounded in the legs, made a forced landing.

The last of the German bombers and their escorts vanished into the thickening mist; the battle of Paris was over. In the course of the afternoon the French fighters had flown 243 sorties and destroyed twenty-six enemy aircraft. Seventeen French aircraft had been lost, with twelve pilots killed.

For the Germans, the results of Operation Paula had been disappointing. The concentrated attacks on thirteen airfields in the Paris area had resulted in the destruction of only sixteen aircraft on the ground, with a further seven damaged. Six runways had been temporarily put out of action, twenty-one vehicles destroyed and thirty-two personnel killed. All the bases attacked were serviceable again within forty-eight hours. The bombers had also attacked twenty-two railway stations and junctions; here, too, repairs were completed by dawn on 4 June. Fifteen factories were hit, but only three suffered more than minor damage.

But the bombs had taken their toll of civilian lives. Two hundred and fifty-four people had been killed, and over six hundred injured. The citizens of Paris screamed for reprisals. Why, they demanded to know, were French bombs not falling on Berlin?

In fact, plans were already being made for an attack on the German capital – using the one and only French aircraft that was capable of getting there.

INTERLUDE: THE FLIGHT OF THE *JULES VERNE*, 7 JUNE 1940

Amid all the chaos and misery of almost continual retreat, there shone deeds of courage and dedication that were to be an inspiration to those who followed in later years, as individual Frenchmen fought their own battle against the floodtide that burst across their land. One such was *Commandant* Daillière, the central figure of one of the most astonishing air dramas of the war.

In October 1939, a month after the outbreak of hostilities, several French naval officers were summoned urgently to Paris to be briefed for a special mission. They had only been in uniform for a few weeks, having been called up with

France's reserve forces when war with Germany seemed inevitable. All had one thing in common: in peacetime, they had formed the crews of the giant Farman and Latecoere transport aircraft which plied the intercontinental air routes between France and her colonies.

In Paris, the officers learned that the French Admiralty had requisitioned a pair of Farman transports belonging to Air France, and that they were to fly these machines on long-range maritime patrol duties over the South Atlantic. Their primary mission was to locate and track the German warships *Admiral Graf Spee* and *Admiral Scheer*, which were threatening the Allied trade routes. For this purpose, the aircraft were to be based in Brazil.

The two machines took off from Bordeaux on 8 October 1939 and headed south. After a non-stop flight of sixteen hours they reached Dakar in West Africa, where they refuelled in readiness for the next leg: the crossing of the Atlantic. Arriving in Brazil late on the eleventh, after fourteen and a half hours over the ocean, they began their operational task almost at once, ranging far out over the sea on search of the elusive warships. Since Brazil was neutral, the aircraft – which were still in Air France colours – carried out their reconnaissance flights under the guise of weather research. Their efforts, however, were in vain, and they were recalled to France in November. One of them skidded off the runway at Dakar and was completely wrecked, although the crew escaped unhurt.

Meanwhile, the French Admiralty had requisitioned three more Air France transports: new Farmans, all factory fresh and named after celebrated French science writers of the nineteenth century – *Jules Verne*, *Camille Flammarion* and *Leverrier*. They were fitted with machine-guns, and in theory at least they could carry three tons of bombs over a range of 3,000 miles. The three aircraft were placed under the command of *Commandant* Daillière, an experienced long-range pilot who had led the transatlantic detachment, and various schemes were put forward for their use during the winter of 1939–40. One such was to employ them in laying magnetic mines in the Gulf of Bothnia, between Finland and Sweden, through which a high proportion of Germany's vital iron ore traffic passed. In the event this scheme came to nothing, although the *Jules Verne* was modified to carry bombs or mines on racks under the wings, the interior of the fuselage being almost entirely taken up by fuel tanks, with only a narrow catwalk from nose to tail. Neither of the other machines was modified in this way, and *Jules Verne* consequently became the only Farman to carry out offensive operations.

Early in 1940, Daillière strongly advocated using the *Jules Verne* to bomb targets in Germany, Berlin being at the top of his list. The French Admiralty, however, refused to agree to such a plan, not only because the bombing of enemy territory was not yet Allied policy, but because Daillière, with his vast experience, was considered too valuable a person to risk his life on a mission of this kind.

Nevertheless, Daillière and his crew carried out many practice bombing missions in the spring of 1940, and on 11 May, the day after the start of the German offensive in the west, they were briefed to carry out their first offensive sortie. At dusk, the *Jules Verne* took off from its base at Lanveoc-Poulmic, on the Cherbourg peninsula, and flew to Aachen, where it dropped a few bombs in the vicinity of the railway station. On the way home it bombed the bridges at Maastricht, over which the German armoured divisions were pouring into the Low Countries. The damage caused in both attacks was negligible. The next mission, on the night of 14 May, was against road junctions on the island of Walcheren, where units of the French Seventh Army – which had advanced deep into Holland – were cut off and isolated.

The third and fourth missions, on 16 and 20 May, were once again flown against rail targets in Aachen. The second of these sorties was particularly exacting for the crew, for the night was brilliantly clear and the German defences were fully alerted. The *Jules Verne* was flying at only 1,200 feet, following the main railway line that led towards its objective, Aachen station, when suddenly the aircraft was caught in a web of searchlights. The big machine was still uncamouflaged and her silver paintwork glittered in the intense light, making her a sitting target.

Although Daillière was aircraft captain, the *Jules Verne* was flown on this occasion by Master Pilot Queugnet, who now took her down to rooftop level and began a series of violent evasive manoeuvres. Daillière, half-blinded by the searchlights, ordered the pilot to make two runs over the station before releasing his bombs. Although the flak was intense, the big aircraft miraculously collected only two splinter holes before making its escape. There was, however, one casualty as a result of this attack: Master Pilot Queugnet, who was so exhausted by the strain of throwing the huge, ponderous machine around the sky at low level that he had to be replaced by Master Pilot Yonnet, who piloted the *Jules Verne* on all her subsequent missions.

During the closing days of May the *Jules Verne* undertook several tactical operations, notably against German armoured columns in the Clair Marais Forest and an important railway junction near St Omer. Dailliére, meanwhile, had been continuing to seek approval for a raid on Berlin, but at the end of May – even with the French armies collapsing on all sides – the government was still reluctant to approve such a step for fear of reprisals. It was only on 4 June, following the large-scale attack on targets in the Paris area, that the French authorities relented and Daillière was ordered to put his plans ito action.

The French Admiralty, which had been the sole authority governing the *Jules Verne*'s operations so far, already possessed a considerable dossier of target photographs and maps of the Berlin area, which Daillière and his crew had memorised thoroughly. By this time the *Jules Verne* and her two sister Farmans had been formed into an official French Navy unit, *Escadrille* B5, which was based at Bordeux-Merignac on the coast, and to achieve maximum surprise Daillière decided to route the flight to Berlin over water for as long as possible, the aircraft flying over the English Channel and the North Sea before turning eastwards across the 'neck' of Denmark, north of Kiel, and approaching the German capital from the north. The attack was to be made at a height of not less than 4,500 feet because of the danger from barrage balloons, and under no circumstances were bombs to be dropped on densely-populated areas.

The *Jules Verne* took off from Merignac on the long outward journey at three o'clock in the afternoon of 7 June, the flight timed so that the aircraft would arrive over Denmark just as darkness was falling. As it lumbered along the Channel coast at 160 miles per hour, labouring under the weight of fuel and bombs it carried, it was fired on several times by French and British warships, who at this stage in the Battle of France understandably considered every aircraft they sighted to be hostile. Fortunately, on this occasion at least, their shooting was poor.

Lieutenant Paul Comet, the *Jules Verne*'s navigator, had no difficulty in following his course. The weather was absolutely clear, and excellent visibility enabled him to pick out the island of Sylt from a considerable distance – an important point, for there were heavy anti-aircraft defences on the island and Comet had been worried in case they strayed over them. But Sylt slid by harmlessly on the right, and the aircraft flew peacefully on.

The wind forecast had been very precise, allowing Comet to work out an exact ground speed, and after crossing Denmark without incident the *Jules Verne* made landfall on the Baltic coast north of Berlin right on schedule. It was only now that the navigator began to experience some difficulty, because heavy cloud had crept over northern Germany, extending down to about 1,000 feet, and it proved impossible to locate some of the planned landmarks. From time to time, Comet saw a lake through a rift in the cloud, but he was unable to make any positive identification. Then, by sheer good luck, he saw a glow in the sky far ahead: it was caused by Berlin's searchlights. The aircraft's approach must have been detected, and the capital's air-raid defences were now on the alert.

Master Pilot Yonnet steered directly towards the probing searchlight beams. As soon as he reached the suburbs, he flew a series of pre-planned courses over the city, designed to make the Germans think that more than one aircraft was involved. The *Jules Verne*'s undersides had now been painted matt black and the Germans seemed completely unable to locate the aircraft, despite the dozens of searchlight beams that swept to and fro across the night sky. As yet, not a single anti-aircraft gun had opened up.

Up in the nose of the aircraft, Daillière and Yonnet were finding it increasingly difficult to see. Apart from the glare of the searchlights, more cloud was beginning to drift over Berlin and in just a few more minutes they would be forced to bomb blindly, with the danger of hitting heavily-populated areas. Daillière therefore ordered the pilot to make for the capital's western suburbs without further delay; intelligence photographs had indicated a cluster of factories in this sector of the city, and these seemed to present the most worthwhile target.

Five minutes later, when he judged that they were directly above the objective – the Farman was fitted with only a rudimentary bomb sight – Daillière released the two-ton bomb load and ordered Yonnet to set course directly for France. The pilot put down the Farman's nose to gain speed and opened the throttles, anxious to get clear of the city's fringes before the flak started to come up. A few moments later, the clouds reflected the orange flashes of the bomb bursts, and then the sky lit up with strings of shellbursts, twinkling above the city. None of the enemy fire came near the Farman.

The homeward flight was made without incident, Yonnet

taking the *Jules Verne* in a straight line across western Germany and the Rhine. The aircraft landed at Orly, near Paris, just as dawn was breaking, its fuel reserves practically exhausted.

The *Jules Verne*'s route to Berlin had taken it over Rostock, the home of the Heinkel aircraft factories, and the crew reported that these had been brilliantly lit. The result was that, on the night of 10 June, the Farman once again set out for Germany, with Rostock as the target. The objective was reached after a trouble-free flight, although the crew spent several uncomfortable minutes flying around in heavy flak before Daillière made a satisfactory bombing run. Several fires were reported in the factory area.

Shortly afterwards, the *Jules Verne* was sent to Istres in southern France to take part in operations against the Italians, who had declared war on 10 June. The first mission from this new base, carried out on 14 June, was against oil storage tanks at Porto Marghera, the port of Venice; eight bombs were dropped and one tank was definitely set on fire. A second mission, against Livorno two nights later, was less successful.

The *Jules Verne*'s last sortie was flown on 18 June, when Daillière and his crew paid a visit to Rome – to drop not bombs but leaflets.

Sadly, the big Farman met an inglorious end. Trapped at Marignane through lack of fuel, it was burned to prevent it from falling into enemy hands. *Commandant* Daillière, who became a member of the Vichy French forces, was eventually transferred to Dakar in West Africa.

One day in 1942, a Martin Maryland bomber bearing Vichy French markings strayed into British airspace at Freetown, Sierra Leone. It was intercepted by RAF Hawker Hurricane fighters, and its pilot ignored their signals to land. The RAF fighters opened fire and shot it down. The body of the pilot was found in the wreckage, a bullet through his head.

Such was the tragic death of *Commandant* Daillière, the

man who, with a small band of gallant comrades, carried the war for the first time to Germany's capital in a small, almost personal gesture of defiance that shone like a beacon through the shame of France's collapse.

Chapter Ten

The pilots assembled in the open air in the freshness of a June dawn, straight from their beds, stretching and yawning, rubbing their hands across stubbled faces. Armstrong saw that Villeneuve had called them all together, Frenchmen and Poles, and knew that something big was in the wind. He was not mistaken, and Villeneuve wasted no time on preliminaries as he stood before them, feet slightly apart, his hands clasped behind his back. Armstrong had noticed that the colonel had taken to adopting this particular stance recently, with his hands hidden from view, and knew why; Villeneuve's hands trembled constantly now, for the twin strains of command and combat had taken their toll. Willpower alone was keeping the man going.

"Gentlemen," he said in a high and clear voice that reached them all, "the *Boches* are on the move again. A few hours ago, they began a massive artillery barrage on the Somme front, stretching from the Channel coast to Laon. First reports indicate that General Besson's Third Army Group is under extreme pressure. The enemy has established a bridgehead on the Somme at St Valery, on the left of the Allied line, and the British 51st Division in that sector is under heavy attack. On the right, other units of the 51st Division, together with our own 31st Alpine Division, are withdrawing to the line of the Bresle river between Eu and Blaugy."

The pilots had brought their maps with them and were hurriedly making pencil marks on them, tracing the rapidly shifting battle front as Villeneuve outlined the situation.

"Although compelled to withdraw in the face of superior forces," Villeneuve continued, "the Allies are contesting every metre of ground and are inflicting substantial casualties on the enemy. However, the Germans have captured two intact railway bridges on the Somme, between Conde and Hangest, and their troops are crossing over in great strength. The situation is very confused and I have no information other than that which I have just given you."

Had he known the true picture, Villeneuve would have been horrified. Pouring across the bridges that had been taken by General Hoth's XV *Panzer* Corps, the German infantry had pushed straight on to attack and overwhelm two Senegalese regiments of the 5th Colonial Division, creating a dangerous gap through which the tanks drove on towards Le Quesnoy. Pausing only to shoot up a few isolated pockets of resistance, the German armour thundered on through Le Quesnoy into the Laudon valley, where they were engaged by a battery of 75-mm guns of the French 72nd Artillery Regiment. Several German tanks were knocked out, but the remainder encircled the artillery battery and destroyed it.

By dawn, the German tanks had advanced so far that they had crossed the *Luftwaffe*'s bomb line, with the consequent danger that they might be attacked in error by their own dive-bombers. Their commander therefore halted them and consolidated his position, waiting for the rest of the offensive to catch up.

The German armour belonged to the 7th *Panzer* Division, and its commander was General Erwin Rommel. Rommel again, that thorn in the Allies' flesh!

By his daring thrust across country, Rommel had made nonsense of the whole defensive policy of the line that had been set up on the Somme, the so-called Weygand Line. This relied not on a continuous front but on a network of 'hedgehogs' dotted over the countryside, each hedgehog being a fortified natural obstacle such as a village, wood or farmhouse, with the defending troops well dug in and supported by mortars, heavy machine-guns and 75-mm artillery pieces, the latter with the task of engaging the enemy tanks over open sights. Wherever possible, each hedgehog was situated in a position that enabled it to provide covering fire for its neighbours, and each was provided with sufficient stores and ammunition to carry on fighting for a time even after it had been surrounded.

Although the Weygand Line had been designed to give some semblance of a defence in depth, it was by no means proof against a strong armoured thrust of the type in which Rommel excelled. It might have been a different story if the line had been backed up by strong forces of French armour and heavy air support, but it had neither. But Weygand had ordered his troops to stand and fight to the death, and in many cases they did precisely that. This time there was no disorganised rabble, streaming away from the front; this time the French were fighting with a valour born of desperation, conscious that they were the last shield between the armoured lance and their country's heart. Time and again, the French gunners refused to abandon their positions, hurling shell after shell at the *Panzers* until the steel tracks ground over them or the *Stukas'* bombs pounded them into the dust. At Amiens and Peronne, they halted the advance of General von Kleist's tanks after only a few miles; only in Rommel's sector was any significant advance made.

But that was enough. Allied reinforcements were on the way in the shape of the Scottish 52nd Lowland Division, which was already beginning to arrive in Normandy, and the 1st Canadian Division was preparing to embark for France from England. It was already clear, thanks to Rommel's daring, that they would be too late.

Larks sang in the early rays of the sun over Le Bourget as Villeneuve addressed his pilots, just as they had sung over the Somme battlefield on a June day a quarter of a century earlier. Their melody formed a background to Villeneuve's voice as he continued his briefing.

132

"Our orders are to put our maximum effort into bomber escort," he told them. "Later, we shall be providing air cover for our Seventh and Tenth Armies and, if necessary, we shall be available for ground attack work."

The latter remark brought audible groans from some of the pilots, who knew the kind of havoc that could be wrought by the German light flak. For fighter pilots, ground strafing was the worst possible job. Villeneuve smiled thinly and held up a hand for silence.

"I said if necessary, gentlemen," he reminded them. "That task will be assigned mainly to the Morane squadrons, whose aircraft, unlike ours, are cannon-armed. I do not think our peashooters would make much impression on the *Boche* tanks."

Villeneuve paused and looked around the assembly, his expression grave. "Make no mistake, gentlemen, we are embarking on what may be the final battle in the struggle for our homeland. Each of us must give of his best, so that no matter what the outcome, men will say that we fought bravely to the end. Frenchmen, Poles, British—" he glanced at Armstrong and at Kalinski, who was standing next to the Englishman "– we are all together in this endeavour. And even if we fail, even if France should fall, we must continue the fight from other shores. There must be no place in our thoughts for the word surrender. That is all; we must now await further orders. Good luck to you all."

They came to attention and saluted him; he returned the gesture, then turned on his heel and walked briskly towards his office. Armstrong was left with the uncomfortable feeling that the Frenchman had just delivered a valedictory address.

"Do you think it's all over, Ken?" Kalinski asked him, as they sat on the grass a while later, chewing rolls and drinking milky coffee out of glass bowls. "Do you really think we've lost? Armstrong shrugged.

"It doesn't look too promising," he admitted. "The trouble is, as I see it, that we've precious little left to fight with. Have you noticed any replacement aircraft and pilots coming our way lately? I haven't."

Kalinski thought for a while, then said quietly: "If France does go down, which seems likely, do you think England will sue for peace?" Armstrong snorted.

"Not on your life! We'll go on fighting, you can bet your bottom dollar! We won't let that little bugger Hitler dictate any more terms to us. Mind you, I'm not sure about this new prime minister of ours, Churchill. He made some awful blunders in the last war, or so I'm told. My father can't stand him. But people reckon he's got staying power, and won't let himself – or his country – be pushed around. Maybe if we'd had somebody like him in charge a few years ago, we wouldn't be in this mess now."

"What will you do?" Kalinski wanted to know. "I mean, if France surrenders. Will you try to get back to England?"

"Too bloody true I will! I have no intention of sitting around waiting to be taken prisoner. There's got to be some way. If France packs it in, I intend to make for the coast, and failing that I'll head south. Try to make Gibraltar, maybe. Of course, the quickest way out would be by air. Steal an aeroplane, perhaps. After all, the French won't have much use for 'em if they aren't fighting the Germans any longer. What about you?"

Kalinski looked at him, and there was a gleam in the Pole's eye. "The idea of England is very appealing, my friend. Most of my Polish comrades think so too. So, before you go off and do something dangerous by yourself, consult with me first. Is that a deal, as the Americans say?"

Armstrong grinned at him. "That's a deal, Stan. Don't get yourself killed in the meantime, though." They shook hands solemnly.

Colonel Villeneuve emerged from his command post and walked towards his aircraft. He was now wearing his flying overall, and he nodded to Armstrong and Kalinski as he went past. "We take off in ten minutes. Tell the others. Our orders are to patrol the battlefront. Nothing more than that."

They climbed away into the blue and gold June morning, heading north towards Amiens. The Hawks were leading, the Polish Caudrons some distance behind, the aircraft rising and falling gently on the currents of warm air. At 15,000 feet they levelled off, on the alert now for signs of danger. Far below their wings the land was speckled with woods, intersected by winding roads and railways joining the towns and villages: Beauvais, Breteuil, Montdidier, and finally Amiens itself, lost in the haze that covered the northern horizon.

Here, though, the air was fresh and clean, with near-perfect visibility for miles. Away to the left was Dieppe, with the Channel gleaming in the rising sun. The Channel! How easy it would be to reach it, Armstrong thought, to fly on for another hundred miles or so, to the Sussex coast, and home.

He tore his gaze from that direction, looking at the flights of aircraft around him, their blue, white and red roundels – the reverse of the RAF's – standing out against their drab camouflage. They were flown by men who had become firm friends, men to whom he had a duty. He would see it through, no matter what. And if his destiny was to end his life among them, so be it.

"Here they come. Messerschmitts, above and to the right. Turn to meet them, and spread out."

Villeneuve's voice set every nerve tingling. A sensation like an electric shock passed through Armstrong's body, then all at once, as usual, he was icily calm, focusing his eyes on the silvery shapes that came tumbling out of the north-eastern sky like hawks stooping for the kill. The two formations closed with phenomenal speed and then they were upon one another, racing through a maze of smoky tracers as they opened fire simultaneously. Armstrong picked an Me 109 and stuck doggedly to his course, firing in short bursts as the enemy fighter filled his windscreen. Suddenly the German pilot's nerve broke and he flicked away to the left, exposing his pale blue belly to Armstrong's fire. Something fell off the 109 and narrowly missed Armstrong's cockpit canopy as it whirled away.

There was no time to see what had happened to the Messerschmitt. The sky was filled with whirling, twisting aircraft. Armstrong climbed hard, trying desperately to get above the meleé?, to arrive at a vantage point from which he could obtain a better tactical picture of the air battle. Over the past weeks he had taught himself a formula: first gain altitude, then pick your target, then hit him in the dive at speed, and get out fast. It seemed to be a recipe for survival.

He saw that he was still accompanied by his two wingmen, which brought considerable relief. At 18,000 feet he turned out of the climb and dipped his wings in succession, looking down to make sure that nothing was climbing after him and his two colleagues. But the sky at this altitude was empty, and he took a few moments to make a careful survey of what was happening below.

Here and there smoke trails twisted down towards the green-and-brown landscape. Looking hard, he saw a couple of parachutes, circular white dots that looked for all the world like nails that someone had studded into the ground. But the nails were drifting, and underneath each one swung a pilot, thanking his God for deliverance, but perhaps wounded, maybe even dying.

Checking his map, he saw that his climb had taken him north of the Somme, well into enemy-held territory. In just a few minutes more he would be over the town of Albert. There was no sign below of any aircraft, either enemy or friendly, and he decided that it was time to head for safer skies. Circling towards the south, with his wingmen sticking to him like glue, he spotted some columns of smoke rising in the distance and drew the attention of the other two pilots to them.

The three Hawks went into a shallow dive, crossing the Somme again. As they flew on, more smoke burst into the sky from the ground, and Armstrong knew that he was witnessing a bombing attack. A couple of minutes later he picked out the aircraft responsible, diving and then climbing steeply above the smoke, and he knew them for what they were. He pressed the radio switch and yelled into the microphone, all R/T procedure forgotten in his sudden excitement.

"All French fighters, concentrate on the Montdidier sector," he cried. "Allied forces under attack by *Stukas*. I repeat, *Stukas* – and with no fighter escort!"

He and his two fellow pilots were going to be first into the battle. They continued their dive, building up their speed, and headed towards the middle of the beehive of enemy dive-bombers. Picking a section of three Junkers 87s that were still flying in formation, preparing to dive on whatever target lay on the ground, they closed in rapidly and opened fire.

The *Stuka* in Armstrong's sights suddenly went into a steep turn, its pilot alerted to the threat by his gunner. It flew straight into the path of Armstrong's bullets. The RAF pilot kept his finger on the trigger and raked the dive-bomber from the yellow spinner at its nose right through to its tail. The long glasshouse cockpit shattered into fragments and then he was streaking over the rapidly disintegrating bomber like a flash of lightning.

He pulled up hard and stall-turned, arrowing down to make a second attack. It was not necessary. The *Stuka*, its pilot probably dead at the controls, was fluttering earthwards like a falling leaf. Two other Ju 87s were going down, the victims of his wingmen, one a ball of blazing fragments, destroyed by the explosion of its own bomb.

Armstrong selected another target, a Stuka that was weaving uncertainly ahead of him. He closed in to point-blank range, ignoring the tracer that sprayed at him from the German's rear gun. For the first time in air combat, he felt a burning, murderous anger against the men he was going to kill. Up to this point his feelings had been dispassionate; he had even felt sorry for the crew member of the Dornier whose remains had been spattered over his fighter weeks earlier. This was something different. He wanted to kill these men, to strew their charred remains over the French countryside. Now it was France; tomorrow it would be England that lay at the mercy of their bombs.

Not if he could help it. Bastards, he thought, and pressed the trigger again, literally chopping the *Stuka* to pieces from a range of fifty yards. The rear gunner was dead, a bloodstained bundle sprawled over his gun. The *Stuka* was in shreds, flames licking back from its engine. The front section of its cockpit canopy flew off and whirled away in the slipstream. The dive-bomber lost speed. Armstrong saw the pilot trying to struggle clear.

Armstrong throttled back. He raised the Hawk's nose a little, put his sights squarely on the luckless German, and squeezed the trigger, intent on blowing the man apart.

Nothing happened. He was out of ammunition. A red veil of rage crossed his vision and he inched towards the *Stuka*. Madness possessed him as it filled the sky ahead. He was going to ram it.

Then the enemy pilot dropped away from the doomed aircraft and reason returned. He hauled on the stick and pulled the Hawk away, averting a collision by a hair's breadth. Sweating and shaking, aching in every limb, he looked down, seeing the German's dark shape tumbling towards the ground. He saw no sign of a parachute.

Suddenly, the sky was full of aircraft as more Hawks and some Caudrons joined the combat. He called up his wingmen and headed for Paris, his presence useless now that he had no bullets left. Behind him, dark columns of smoke, like tombstones, marked the last fiery plunge of a dozen *Stukas*. The remainder dropped their bombs haphazardly and fled, harried by the French fighters, who only gave up the chase when they were forced to do so through shortage of fuel and ammunition.

The destruction of the dive-bombers was the single biggest success of 5 June, a day in which the French fighter groups flew 438 sorties and claimed 40 enemy aircraft for the loss of 15 of their own. In the afternoon, as Colonel Villeneuve had predicted, the cannon-armed Morane units were ordered to carry out ground-attack missions, and at 1400 six aircraft made a low-level cannon attack on a column of about seventy enemy tanks; one tank was knocked out but all the Moranes were hit and two of their pilots wounded.

At 1700 eight more Moranes set out to attack the same column. This time ten Me 109s were waiting for them and a fierce dogfight flared up over Royes, in the course of which two Moranes and two 109s were destroyed. The last fighter ground-attack sortie of the day was carried out between 2000 and 2030 by nine Moranes escorted by nine D. 520s of GC I/3 and II/7. The pilots of I/3 shot down four Me 109s and a Henschel 126 observation aircraft; one French pilot was shot down and killed and a second wounded.

It was not the first hectic air battle involving I/3 that day. Earlier, at 1705, six aircraft had been sent out on an air cover mission in the Braye-sur-Somme sector. They were accompanied by eight more D.520s of GC II/7, flying at a higher altitude. At 25,000 feet over Compiègne the latter were suddenly ambushed by fifteen Me 109s; twenty-five more enemy fighters circled watchfully at a distance, ready to pick off any stragglers. The 109s swept through the French formation in a dive, shooting down two D.520s and badly damaging a third on their first pass.

The three pilots of II/7's lower flight turned to meet the attackers head-on and one of them, *Sous-Lieutenant* Pomier-Layragues, set a 109 on fire with a short burst. The pilot bailed out; he was *Hauptmann* Werner Moelders, commander of a squadron of the elite German fighter unit, JG 53. At that time his score stood at twenty-five French and British aircraft destroyed. Taken prisoner by French artillerymen, Moelders at once asked if he might be permitted to meet the man who had shot him down.

He was too late. Even as the German ace parachuted to earth, Pomier-Layragues found himself in a desperate single-handed fight against four Me 109s. He shot one of them down, but in the following moments his fighter was torn apart by the shells of six more Messerschmitts. A ball of fire, it crashed in the suburbs of Marissel and exploded. The pilot had not bailed out.

At Le Bourget, Armstrong and his fellow pilots flew two more missions in the course of the day, both escorting Potez 63s which were assigned to photograph the movement of German forces across the Somme bridges. During the second mission, the French aircraft were attacked by ten Me 109s and 110s, which broke through to shoot down the Potez in flames.

A swirling air battle developed, with the French and German pilots striving to gain a height advantage. In the end, from the ground, the twisting fighters seemed no more than silvery midges against the sky's deep blue.

German troops paused in their march to watch the combat, hearing the scream of tortured aero-engines and the distant rattle of machine-guns. In the midst of the mêlée they saw a sudden flare, a starburst of light, followed by a pencil-line of smoke that raced towards the earth. The doomed aircraft fell arrow-straight, its engine still howling. It fell for an eternity, the noise of its passing growing louder with every moment, until it streaked out of sight behind a clump of trees on the horizon, the point of its impact marked by a great geyser of smoke and earth.

Troops who reached the spot found only a smoking crater, with a few scraps of twisted metal lying around. Of the pilot, not a relic remained.

It was, perhaps, the way in which Colonel Pierre Villeneuve would have wished to die.

Chapter Eleven

The battle in the north continued its inexorable course. On 6 June General von Kleist renewed his advance, but once again the French stopped him. One of his armoured corps had over half its tanks disabled after two days of fighting. Once again, it was Rommel who kept the offensive going. Exploiting the gap he had created, he raced on to cover another thirty miles, advancing as far as Forges-les-Eaux on the Beauvais-Dieppe road and slicing the French Tenth Army in two as he did so. On the 7th his meteoric progress continued as he drove the centre of the Tenth Army before him in what was fast becoming a rout, and at 0200 on the eighth, after a brief halt, his tanks reached Elbeuf on the River Seine.

In the picturesque villages, many inhabitants gazed in bewilderment as the *Panzers* rolled through, unable to comprehend the speed with which disaster was overtaking them. Only a few hours before, they had cheered and thrown bouquets of flowers at the men of their own 3rd Armoured Division, now pulling back over the Seine. Such was the confusion that in Elbeuf a woman came up to Rommel's command vehicle and asked the general if he was English.

Rommel's dash did not succeed in securing the Seine bridges, which were blown one after the other. The town of Rouen, however, fell that same morning to General von Hartlieb's 5th *Panzer* Division, the tanks and personnel carriers rumbling in a long column up Autoroute 28 and entering the town unmolested. Meanwhile, on Rommel's other flank, and infantry corps under General Erich von Manstein had succeeded in forcing a passage through to the lower Seine.

The German drive to the Seine, and the splitting of the French Tenth Army, had effectively sealed off the French Ninth Corps – which included the British 51st Highland Division – in the Rouen-Dieppe pocket, with their backs to the sea, and their encirclement was completed on the 9th when the 5th and 7th *Panzer* Divisions swung north-westwards from the Seine. The next morning, Rommel and von Hartlieb launched a concerted attack on Ninth Corps, which had set up a hasty line of defence around the perimeter of St Valery-en-Caux, where the 51st Division and the remnants of the French forces expected to be evacuated by sea, as had happened at Dunkirk. This, however, was prevented by the fog and by the Germans themselves, who by noon on the 11th were in a position to shell both the Allied ships offshore and the beaches at St Valery.

The Highlanders and most of the French now had less than half a day's rations left. On the morning of the 12th, General Ihler, the Ninth Corps commander, ordered the French forces at St Valery to surrender, and although this raised bitter protests from the Highlanders, who were prepared to fight on, they were compelled to do likewise soon afterwards. Over 8,000 British troops fell into the German net; the total bag of Allied troops that day was 40,000, including no fewer than twelve generals.

Rommel's tanks clattered into Le Havre on the morning of 14 June. There they rested for forty-eight hours before pushing on towards Cherbourg, covering as much as 150 miles in a single day. There was no longer any opposition, and on 19 June Rommel accepted Cherbourg's surrender. For the incredible 7th *Panzer* Division, which alone had taken close on a 100,000 prisoners in its headlong dash from the Meuse to the sea, the Battle of France was over.

Meanwhile, on 9 June, the German Army Group A had

attacked on the River Aisne, the weight of its offensive falling on the newly-formed French Fourth Army Group, comprising the Second, Fourth and Sixth Armies and commanded by General Huntziger. Ever since the German breakthrough on the Meuse, the French Second Army had been under relentless pressure, striving to hold some sort of line between the Bar and the Meuse and so prevent the outflanking of the Maginot Line. Losses were heavy, and reserves were continually being drained to make good the attrition. Despite this, the Second Army had been compelled to withdraw during the last week of May, and as a consequence part of the Maginot defences had to be abandoned.

Now, effective from 6 June, Huntziger's new Army Group – into which the last of the reserves had been poured – was given the task of holding the Aisne from Montmedy to Attichy. Three days later, it received the full weight of the German attack, which was carried out by the armoured groups of Generals Heinz Guderian and Ewald von Kleist, the latter having been switched eastwards.

This time, the infantry were to go in first and secure bridgeheads across the Aisne before the armour was committed. The first assault fell between Neufchatel and Attigny. The French resisted furiously, and by the end of the day the Germans had succeeded in establishing only one small bridgehead. The Germans made determined attacks on the French 14th Division – commanded by a fine officer, General de Lattre de Tassigny – through the murk that was a mixture of mist and the effects of smoke shells, lying like a veil across the valley, but the French broke them all and took 800 prisoners into the bargain.

French losses, however, had been severe, and it was plain that Army Group Four would not be able to stem the German breakthrough for much longer. That night, Guderian pushed armour into the solitary bridgehead, and the next morning elements of 1st *Panzer* Division probed through the French advance positions supported by heavy air strikes. Village after village went up in flames, and although the tanks made slow progress, the defenders were gradually compelled to withdraw. Then, in the early afternoon, the *Panzers* encountered units of the French 3rd Armoured Division, comprising ten large 'B' tanks and two battalions of Hotchkiss. German reconnaissance aircraft had warned of the approach of the French armour, and when the tanks reached Juneville, the German anti-tank gunners were ready for them. Six Hotchkiss were knocked out in as many minutes, and although the heavier armoured vehicles made some progress, the French counter-attack – which lacked both artillery and air support – soon petered out.

The situation continued to deteriorate, and in the early hours of 11 June the French Second and Fourth Armies began to disengage, moving back through the forest of Belval towards the river Marne. The manoeuvre was carried out with extreme difficulty, for by this time two *Panzer* corps had crossed the Aisne and were pushing southwards at speed, trapping some French units and destroying them. It was clear now that French resistance on the Aisne was practically at an end; by nightfall on the 11th the German armour had reached Reims, and a few hours later Guderian's tanks took Chalons-sur-Marne, establishing a bridgehead on the river.

With Rouen captured in the west and the Marne crossed in the east, Paris was now threatened from west and north, with the leading German forces only fifty miles from the capital. Immediately north of Paris, bitter fighting raged in the forest of Compiègne, where the 11th 'Iron' Division sacrificed itself to buy time while the Seventh Army fell back to the Oise. In Paris itself the thunder of distant gunfire could be clearly heard, and the roads leading south were crowded with the inevitable tide of refugees – among it the French Government, which was departing for a safer location at Tours. On the 11th, aware that there was no hope of defending the capital, General Weygand declared Paris an open city.

Meanwhile, the French fought to hold their last line of defence on the lower Seine. Weygand had committed all his available reserves to the battle, including two fresh divisions from North Africa. At the same time, the first contingent of a new British Epeditionary Force – the 52nd Lowland Division and part of the 1st Canadian – was landed at Cherbourg under the command of General Alan Brooke. A brigade of the Lowland Division was immediately sent up to bolster the French line at Evreux, but when Brook arrived at the French GHQ on 12 June, with no clear idea of the true situation, he was horrified to find that the French position was quite untenable. He at once contacted the War Office and gave his views, and on the 13th – after Churchill had intervened – he was ordered to prepare the withdrawal and evacuation of all British forces from France.

By nightfall on the 13th, the French forces in the west – the Seventh and Tenth Armies and the Army of Paris, the latter formed originally to defend the capital to the last – were all in reatreat towards the Loire. That same evening, units of the German Eighteenth Army came within sight of the Eiffel Tower.

At 0340 the next morning, a lone German motorcyclist roared across the deserted Place Voltaire, circled and went back the way he had come. As the hours went by, detachments of German troops began to appear all over the capital. Loudspeaker cars toured the streets, warning what was left of the population to stay indoors and await further instructions. Nevertheless, as the morning wore on, a few inhabitants began to trickle into the streets, braving a thin drizzle to watch the seemingly endless column of German troops, armour and transport that rumbled southwards across Paris.

At 0930, the German flag broke over the Arc de Triomphe. Fifteen minutes later, the hard-bitten, veteran troops of the German 8th Infantry Division marched down the Champs Elysées in a triumphal victory parade. As the field-grey columns passed the Tomb of the Unknown Warrior, with its Eternal Flame, they saluted. It was as much a gesture of total, overwhelming victory as one of homage.

At six-thirty that evening, German soldiers clustered around the Arc de Triomphe like peacetime tourists were astonished to see two elderly Frenchmen marching towards them in full-dress uniform, complete with swords. They were Edmond Ferrand and Charles Gaudin, both veterans of the 1914–18 war and both holding the honoured position of Guardians of the Flame. Instinctively, for they were soldiers with their own pride, who recognised the pride of others, the Germans snapped to attention as the two men solemnly extinguished the Flame that had burned without interruption for almost twenty years. Then Ferrand and Gaudin marched away, the tears glistening on their cheeks in the evening sunlight.

Chapter Twelve

They had been on the move for days now, leapfrogging from one airstrip to another, always heading south towards Provence and the Alpes Maritimes, where the French Army of the Alps had faced a new enemy since 10 June, when the Italian dictator Mussolini, eager for a share of the spoils now that the victory of his German ally was assured, had declared war on the Allies. Thirty-two Italian divisions that had concentrated on France's Alpine Front moved forward to the attack, confident of overwhelming the thinly-spaced French defences by sheer weight of numbers.

They were destined to receive a harsh rebuff. When General Weygand had called for "one last battle to save honour" with the French armies in the north collapsing, the Alpine Front had been furthest from his mind. Yet it was here, in the snow and the rarified air of the mountains, that the battle was fought.

The airfield at Luc-en-Provence was packed with aircraft. As well as the surviving Hawks, flown in by Armstrong and his fellow pilots, there were Morane 406s, Dewoitine D.520s, and a variety of types belonging to the French Naval Air Arm: American-built Chance Vought 156 single-engined attack bombers and Bloch 151 fighters. Some of the latter were running up their engines before setting out on patrol and Armstrong watched them idly. He was stretched out on the parched grass near the airfield's command post, stripped to the waist in the heat, playing a desultory game of chess with Kalinski, who unlike Armstrong was very good at it.

"There is talk of an armistice," Kalinski commented suddenly as he pondered his next move.

"What?" Armstrong looked at the Pole, startled.

"An armistice," Kalinski repeated. "Everyone is talking about it. I'm surprised you haven't heard. Apparently there's quite a strong pro-armistice lobby in the French Government, led by some ancient warrior called Marshal Pétain. The alternative, of course, is to carry on the fight from their North African colonies, but with the Italians in the war they might have their work cut out to hold on to them. One thing's certain, though; they are done for here."

Armstrong nodded. The effect on French morale that had accompanied the news of the fall of Paris a day earlier had been little short of catastrophic, and that very morning – 15 June – word had also arrived that the fortress of Verdun, that symbol of dogged resistance where the flower of the French Army had been sacrificed in 1916, had been captured after less than a day's fighting. There was also a strong rumour that German tanks had reached Dijon on the upper Seine; if it were true, the Maginot Line would now be isolated, together with its defenders – some 400,000 men who would have been far better employed elsewhere.

Armstrong wished, now, that he had severed his connection with the French and made his way to the Cherbourg peninsula, from which the last British troops in France were being evacuated. He had suggested this to Kalinski, who had reluctantly decided against it. Although Polish personnel from other units had already taken ship for England, their aircraft having been destroyed or abandoned in the fighting in the north, Kalinski's small command was still pretty much intact, and he had no orders to cease fighting. So Armstrong had stayed too; if the worst came to the worst, and the French unexpectedly threw in the towel, he would head for Toulon or Marseille. There were bound to be British ships there, sent in to evacuate British nationals.

The Bloch 151s, nine aircraft in all, were taxying out for

take-off. Kalinski, the chessboard momentarily abandoned, watched them too. Suddenly, the Pole gave an exclamation and pointed towards the east. Armstrong followed his gaze and picked out half a dozen dots, growing larger by the second. Whatever they were, they were flying low, and they were heading straight for the airfield.

"Italians!" exclaimed Kalinski, who had phenomenal eyesight. "Fiat CR.42s . . . I suggest we get under cover, my friend!"

Without another word he jumped up and made for a slit trench which had been dug about fifty yards away. Armstrong grabbed his shirt and followed him, one eye on the incoming aircraft. He could identify them now: Fiat CR.42s, biplane fighters, the equivalent of the RAF's Gloster Gladiator.

Breathing hard, he jumped into the trench and cautiously raised his head. The first flight of four Bloch 151s had just got airborne and were beginning to climb away when the Fiats fell on them, their machine-guns stuttering. One Bloch was hit immediately just as its wheels were coming up; it turned over on its back, dived into the ground and exploded. A second, riddled with bullets and its pilot wounded, crash-landed in a cloud of dust; a third crashed just off the end of the runway, its pilot miraculously crawling unhurt from the pile of wreckage. The fourth flew slap through the middle of the enemy fighters, pulled up in a steep climb and turned back towards the airfield.

Armstrong and Kalinski ducked down into their trench as the Italian fighters raced across the field, firing at a group of Vought 156 bombers. Six of them went up in flames. Then the CR.42s turned and came back to concentrate on the second flight of Blochs, which were just lifting away from the runway.

Suddenly, a shadow flitted over the slit trench, its passage accompanied by the scream of an engine. Startled, the two men looked up and saw a Dewoitine D.520, flying very fast, closing in on the two Fiats at the rear of the enemy formation. Within seconds, both of them were spinning down in flames.

Spellbound, Armstrong and Kalinski watched as the French fighter went unhesitatingly after the remaining Fiats, whose pilots, abandoning their pursuit of the Blochs as they became aware of the danger bearing down on them from astern, scattered to left and right. The Dewoitine shot the tail off one of them and another, its pilot making a desperate attempt to escape at low level, flew into the ground, his aircraft cartwheeling across the airfield in a ball of debris, smoke and blazing fuel. The other two got away, dwindling in the distance.

There was no time to admire the French pilot's performance. As the Dewoitine broke off its chase and came back to the airfield to land, an orderly came running out of the command post, waving his arms. He skidded to a halt beside the slit trench and looked down at its occupants, saluting awkwardly.

"The Navy reports enemy bombers approaching from the sea," he told them breathlessly. "Heading this way. At least twenty."

Armstrong and Kalinski leaped from the trench, the RAF pilot hurriedly pulling on his shirt. "Very well," he said. "Let the other pilots know, quickly."

He looked around. Although the Fiats' strafing attack had caused a good deal of damage to the aircraft on the far side of the aerodrome the Hawks and the Polish Caudrons were untouched. Moreover, they had just been rearmed and refuelled. Of the Bloch 151s that had just taken off, there was no sign; Armstrong assumed that they had streaked off in pursuit of the fleeing pair of Italian fighters.

There was no time to lose. He ran towards the nearest Hawk and saw that the French ground crew, who had been lying prone on the ground during the attack, had anticipated his intentions. The fitter was already in the cockpit, and the engine coughed into life as Armstrong arrived at the wing. The mechanic jumped out on the opposite side, leaving the pilot free to take his place.

Armstrong waved the ground crew clear and eased open the throttle, strapping himself in as he taxied towards the runway and leaving the cockpit canopy open for the moment. He turned the fighter's nose into the light breeze and opened the throttle wide, giving the control column a gentle nudge forward to lift the tail as the Hawk gathered speed. Then he was airborne and climbing hard to the south, to where the Mediterranean sparkled beyond the Côte d'Azur. A quick glance astern told him that more fighters were following and he looked ahead again, scanning the sky.

He saw the anti-aircraft bursts first, clusters of white puffs against the blue backdrop as French warships out to sea hammered away at the incoming bombers far above. It was a few moments more before he picked out the aircraft; there did not seem to be more than a dozen of them, flying in two tight boxes at about 15,000 feet. They were still over the sea as he crossed the coast, heading out over the Îles d'Hyeres. A few moments later they passed over the top of him, still a couple of thousand feet higher up.

Armstrong continued his climb until his altimeter showed 5,000 metres – about 16,500 feet – and then turned in astern of the enemy formation, flying through a spread of spent anti-aircraft bursts as he did so. He could see the bombers clearly now: they were twin-engined aircraft with twin fins, and he identified them at once as Fiat BR.20s.

Remembering to close the cockpit hood, he put the Hawk into a shallow dive and gradually overhauled the bomber on the left of the rearmost formation. Fire was beginning to come at him from the dorsal gun positions of several aircraft; he ignored it and concentrated on his target. The Fiat's wings and upper fuselage were painted in a mottled camouflage scheme of light and dark brown; its engine cowlings were yellow and there was a white band around its rear fuselage. Its wings bore the black-and-white insignia of Fascist Italy.

Armstrong could clearly see the white face of the Italian gunner, peering at him over his oxygen mask as he went on firing at him with his single 12.7-mm machine-gun. The bullets passed harmlessly below the Hawk. Making quite sure of his aim, Armstrong opened fire, pushing on the rudder bar so that the fighter's nose yawed from side to side, traversing the nose to allow his bullets to rake the bomber from wingtip to wingtip. The effect was immediate and dramatic. White smoke burst from both the Fiat's engines and streamed back, enveloping the Hawk.

Armstrong continued firing at the shadowy outline of the bomber, and a moment later the smoke became shot with flame as the Fiat's wing fuel tanks caught fire. The aircraft entered a steep diving turn, jettisoning its bombs as it did so. It fell towards the sea, trailing sheets of flame, and a solitary parachute broke away from it. Armstrong hoped that it was the rear gunner, a brave man who had gone on firing at him until the end.

Tearing his gaze from the doomed aircraft, he looked around him. The fight had taken him below the Italian formation, which was now being engaged by more fighters. He pulled up steeply, narrowly avoiding a diving D.520 as he did so, and found himself under a Fiat's sky-blue belly. He put a two-second burst into it, the Hawk hanging on its propeller, then the fighter stalled and dropped away. Dust and other associated debris, the accumulation of several days, whirled around his head as he regained control. He swore, making a mental note to have a word with the ground crew about keeping the cockpit clean, then realised that this was not his usual aircraft.

He was well below the battle now, and could see that the unescorted bombers were taking a terrible mauling. One dropped ponderously past him, turning slowly over and over as it fell; another had turned out of formation and was being harried by three fighters as it dived away over the Mediterranean.

Armstrong decided to try his radio, to see if the Command Post had received word of any more Italian bombers heading in from the sea. But the set was dead; few radios worked now. The Air Force logistical system had broken down and necessary spare parts were not reaching the squadrons. The mechanics worked valiantly, patching up serviceable aircraft with bits and pieces salvaged from wrecked ones, but even these were in short supply.

His engine was beginning to sound alarmingly rough, and the oil temperature was rising. It was time to head for base; the others were quite capable of handling the Italians, most of whom in any case had jettisoned their bomb loads haphazardly and were heading flat out for home. One crew, however, was made of sterner stuff than the rest; the pilot pressed on with his mission, which was to bomb the airfield at Luc, and was shot down in sight of it by D.520s that had been patrolling Marseille. The Italians all bailed out safely and were dined by the French officers before being whisked off to captivity.

Armstrong reached Luc without incident, despite the smoke that was now streaming from under the Hawk's engine cowling, and taxied to a stop near the hangars. The mechanics stripped off the fighter's engine cowling, looked at the oiled-up mess underneath and shook their heads sorrowfully. "It will be at least a day, *mon Capitaine*, before we can make this machine ready for flight once more," the senior NCO told the pilot.

"I'll settle for this afternoon," Armstrong said brusquely. "I feel we are going to need it." He was right.

A hundred miles north-east of Luc, high in the Alpes Maritimes, a series of key positions was manned by crack French alpine troops. Morale among these soldiers was excellent, despite the depressing military situation, and every man was determined to do his utmost to stop the Italians in their tracks. Before the Italians could make progress to north or south, they knew that they would have to break the French at two places, the Col d'Enclave and the Col du Bonhomme. For them, it was to be a costly undertaking.

The Col d'Enclave was occupied by a single company of *Chasseurs* under the command of Lieutenant Armand Bulle. They had decided to set up an obervation post on the Tête de Balleval, a lofty position that offered an unparalleled view of the surrounding terrain. The post was established at noon on 15 June, Bulle and a small party of skiers making a series of trips in dense fog to deposit weapons and supplies on the peak. As they continued with their task, they heard the noise of gunfire echoing from the mountain walls; it seemed to be coming from the Bellegard strongpoint, the main defensive position before the Col d'Enclave, which was held by fifty men under the command of Bulle's friend, Lieutenant Castex. Attacked by a force five times their number, the French put up a spirited resistance, but it was hopeless. Castex was killed, and threequarters of his men were soon casualties.

When the fog lifted in the early afternoon, Bulle saw to his horror that Bellegarde was in enemy hands, and that Italian reinforcements were pouring into the position. From his vantage point, he immediately signalled the French artillery, which opened up a devastating and accurate barrage on the enemy troops milling around on the mountain slopes. A detachment of Italian soldiers tried to advance on Bulle's position, but they were decimated by mortar and machine-gun fire.

Then came the blow. The artillery commander reported that his guns had run out of ammunition, and that promised supplies had not arrived. Through his binoculars, Bulle saw the Italians preparing for what looked like a massed attack. Taking out a message pad, he wrote:

My section is in position on the approaches to the Col d'Enclave. The enemy have overwhelmed de Castex and

154

have encircled the Seloges strongpoint. In the event of no further orders from you, my company will continue to prevent a passage through the Col d'Enclave. We do not have many men, but we shall hold on. As long as have a single bullet left, no enemy soldier will break through the Col. Long live eternal France!

Meanwhile, Bulle's men, in the certainty that they were going to die, had been hastily scribbling last letters to their families with fingers that were numb with cold. Bulle placed them in a satchel, together with his message, and handed the bag to one of his *chasseurs*, Corporal Blanc Ovide, the best skier in the company. Bulle seized the NCO by the hand. "Go, Ovide," he said. "Go like the wind! And may God go with you."

The men watched anxiously as Ovide sped away on his skis, manoeuvring skilfully to avoid the enemy bullets that kicked up spurts of snow at his heels, heading down the valley towards the French command post. Then, as the messenger disappeared from sight, Bulle and the others turned to face the enemy and prepared to sell their lives dearly.

The Italians came in a frontal attack, floundering through the snow in a dense wave, coming on in the senseless manner of an infantry assault in the earlier war, and dying in the same way. Mortar bombs and machine-gun bullets cut great swathes in their ranks. Blood flowed across the snow, and flocks of chamois, the agile mountain goats, lent an incongruous note to the battle as they bounded across the bodies of dead and dying men, fleeing in terror from the storm of fire that had turned their mountain home into a slaughterhouse.

From his observation post, Bulle suddenly spotted a party of Italians attempting to work their way along a ledge below the French position, protected from overhead fire by a rocky outcrop.

Attaching a rope around his waist, the lieutenant ordered his men to lower him over the side until he was dangling

155

in space with a clear view of the infiltrators. Bulle raked the ledge with his sub-machine gun, taking the Italians completely by surprise; only three of them managed to scramble clear, and they were knocked out by a grenade tossed from above.

Meanwhile, it had taken Corporal Blanc Ovide half an hour to reach the command post in the valley, where he encountered Major Ferrier, the commander of that particular sector. Ferrier read Bulle's report, asked a few questions of Ovide, then said decisively:

"They must hold on. Reinforcements are on the way, but they will not be here until tomorrow. They must hold on at all costs."

Although he had not shared the information with anyone else, Ferrier knew that an armistice was in the offing, and that it could come about in a week or perhaps even less. He was determined that the Italians were not going to be in possession of French territory in his sector when it happened. He turned to a signaller who was manning a bank of telephones.

"Lemaitre," he said, "can you open a line to the Alpine Air Operations Zone?"

The man looked surprised. "But, sir, there is one open already. It is just that we have not used it because there has been no sign of the Italian Air Force in this sector, and therefore no need for air cover."

"Well, we have need of it now," Ferrier remarked grimly. "Get on to Air Zone HQ and ask them for as many aircraft as they can spare. I want the Italians attacked and attacked again before nightfall. I want them frightened to move out of their foxholes. We might yet save the skins of Bulle and his men. As for you, Ovide, you have done well. You are overdue for food and rest. Go and get some of both."

The messenger drew himself to attention. "Sir, with respect, my place is with my comrades. Do I have your permission to rejoin them?"

Ferrier looked at him for a moment, then nodded. "Very

well, Corporal, you may go. Tell Lieutenant Bulle that help is on the way."

I only hope to God that it will be in time, he said to himself, as he watched Ovide's retreating back. He shook his head wonderingly, asking himself why, with men such as that, France lay amid the wreckage of defeat. But he already knew the answer, and it had nothing to do with the fighting men.

Ferrier's request for air assistance reached Luc in the middle of the afternoon, and plunged the airfield into a whirlpool of activity as every available aircraft was made ready for the mission. Leaving one battle flight of six Dewoitines for airfield defence in case the *Regia Aeronautica* attempted further attacks, the total came to six Hawks, four Caudrons and eight Moranes. The latter were to go in first, attacking the Italian posts with their cannon, followed by the Hawks. The Caudrons, much to the disgust of their pilots, were assigned a top-cover role as a defence against any possible interference by Italian fighters, but if the Italian Air Force failed to show up Armstrong felt certain that the Poles would find something to shoot at.

The Alps made a breathtaking sight as the formation climbed steadily towards their peaks, the Hawks and Caudrons following the Moranes, whose pilots knew their way around the area. The mountains soared up to 10,000 feet and more, their rock walls intersected by winding roads and rivers; away to the left Armstrong could see a big lake, glittering in the sun. The river that it fed, his map told him, was the Durance, whose waters wound across Provence before joining those of the Rhône.

The RAF pilot was leading the Hawk formation, the French pilots – two of whom were replacements – having readily given way to his experience. Ahead of him, the Moranes flew at a slightly lower altitude, their wingtips almost scraping the snow-covered mountain peaks, or so it seemed from higher up. He followed their every movement

157

as they turned into a high pass – the col they were looking for – seeing their shadows skip across the snow.

Up ahead, orange smoke drifted from a ridge, marking the position of the beleaguered French troops. The Moranes leapfrogged over it and Armstrong saw puffs of smoke dancing away in their slipstream as they opened fire on a target which, for the moment, was invisible to him. Then he was leading his own formation over the French positions, and suddenly, in the adjacent valley, he saw the Italians – dark groups of men and vehicles, silhouetted against the snowy landscape.

The Moranes had completed their attack and were climbing away, leaving the way clear for the Hawks. Some groups of Italians were scattering in search of cover; others stood their ground and fired back. The Hawks' machine-gun fire tore them to shreds. Further down the valley, some trucks were burning, having fallen victim to the Moranes' cannon. Armstrong fired a burst at some that seemed to be intact, then he was tearing overhead, pulling hard back on the stick to avoid a mountain face that loomed up ahead. The Hawk shot vertically into the sky like a stone from a catapult and Armstrong allowed himself to gain a couple of thousand feet of height before rolling out of the climb and turning back the way he had come. Amid these towering peaks there was precious little room for manoeuvre, and none at all for mistakes.

He saw thankfully that the other Hawks had all come through unscathed. They had made their attacks individually and were now climbing up to join him in line astern. Looking up, he caught sight of the Polish fighters crossing from left to right, and grinned as he pictured Kalinski fuming in his cockpit.

The Moranes were a couple of miles ahead, already turning in to make their second strafing run. He saw them pass by on the left, entering a shallow dive, and saw too that this time the Italian defences had woken up. Tracers rose to meet the French fighters, and one of them was hit;

it rose in a steep climb, trailing a thread of smoke, then veered sharply to the right and plunged into a mountain slope in a gush of flame and debris.

He stood the Hawk on its wingtip, turning steeply over the French position, then levelled out, following the remaining Moranes. Almost at once, he saw that most of the Italian fire was coming from two heavy machine-gun positions placed close together on a small plateau above the valley floor, from where they could give covering fire to the troops attacking Bulle's defences. He placed his sights on the right-hand position, instinctively hunching up in the cockpit as tracer came at him like red sleet, and squeezed the Hawk's twin triggers. His bullets sent up a spray of powdered snow as they danced over the enemy position, and the gun abruptly ceased firing. He knew that the other Hawk pilots, following close behind, would complete the job and wipe out the other gun.

He used up the rest of his ammunition on a group of infantry dashing across the valley and then climbed out of danger, going up to 15,000 feet, well clear of the peaks. The other Hawks climbed up and formated on him one by one, the pilots waving, and together they set course for base. The Polish Caudrons, their pilots amazingly obeying orders for once, slid into position on the left of the Hawk formation.

It grew perceptibly warmer as the fighters descended towards Luc, and Armstrong did not envy the troops who had to live and fight in that freezing mountain fastness. The French would have to hold on for at least another night before they were replaced by fresh soldiers.

Hold on they did, through a bitter night in which the temperature fell to twenty below. Snow, icy wind and hunger were beginning to take their toll of the French defenders, crouching in holes hacked from the ice with only tent canvas for protection. There was sporadic firing during the night, but it died away in the early hours; the Italians were in no position to mount a co-ordinated

159

assault in the wake of the air attacks, which had cost them considerable casualties, and at dawn a strange calm hung over the embattled slopes.

Lieutenant Bulle knew, though, that his men, exhausted as they were, could not remain in their positions for much longer. The problem was to get them out of their foxholes; any movement was likely to attract enemy fire. In the end, Bulle set off down the mountain alone, making use of the scant available cover, and after an hour of strenuous effort he reached another defensive position a thousand feet lower down. He had drawn no enemy fire at all, which encouraged him to try to withdraw the other *chasseurs* singly. Those left on the peak would continue to lay down fire on the Italians, and by the time the last man was pulled out the promised reinforcements would hopefully have arrived.

One by one, Bulle's men scrambled down to safety. It was eight hours before the last *chasseur* evacuated the observation post, and before he did so, he was able to shake hands with the first of the replacement troops, fresh and fit and well-armed.

Later that morning, under a mantle of fog, Armand Bulle's weary company was at last relieved. They sang as they marched off down the valley, each man to face his own uncertain future.

Chapter Thirteen

In the afternoon of the day following the attack in the Alps, Armstrong and the other Hawk pilots – who had been on alert since dawn – were dozing in the powerful sunshine when the sudden thunder of aero-engines brought them wide awake. Some of the French jumped to their feet, expecting an enemy air attack, but Armstrong knew that the sound was not made by any Italian aircraft.

Shading his eyes against the sun, he watched as six twin-engined bombers roared overhead in two tight sections of three. They were Vickers Wellingtons. One by one, they peeled off and made their approach to land, their Bristol Hercules radial engines burbling as the pilots throttled back.

Armstrong waited until the bombers had taxied to their dispersals on the far side of the airfield, and then, overcome by curiosity, he grabbed a bicycle and pedalled off across the field to see what was going on. By the time he reached the bombers their crews had disembarked. Throwing his bicycle aside, he sauntered up to the man who was obviously in charge and prepared to intruduce himself.

The man was in deep conversation with some crew members, and his back was towards Armstrong. Suddenly he turned and peered hard at the newcomer, who stopped dead in his tracks as mutual recognition dawned. A moment later, the two men were slapping each other heartily on the back while the other crew members looked on curiously.

"Well, I'm damned!" Armstrong exclaimed. "David Pittaway. What the devil are you doing here?"

Pittaway was a New Zealander. In October 1939, Armstrong had accompanied him on a hair-raising daylight bombing mission to the German naval base of Wilhelmshaven, a sortie that had cost the squadron nine Wellingtons out of twelve. Both men had been injured when their Wellington had crash-landed back at base, having survived repeated fighter attacks.

Pittaway had been a flying officer then, a florid-faced, happy-go-lucky type who had appeared not to have a care in the world. His face was much more serious now, and when he stripped off his Mae West lifejacket Armstrong saw that he had risen to the rank of squadron leader.

"I might ask you the same thing," Pittaway said, in response to Armstrong's question. "But come over here, and I'll tell you all about it."

He took Armstrong by the elbow and steered him off to one side.

"We've got a bit of a show on tonight," he said quietly. "We're off to bomb the Ansaldo aircraft factory at Genoa. As a matter of fact we were going to do it a few days ago; we actually got as far as La Vallon, on the other side of Marseille, and were all set to go when the French commandant got cold feet and had lorries driven onto the runway to prevent us from taking off. It seemed that a civilian deputation had turned up with a fistful of protests at our presence; they were scared stiff that the Eyeties would carry out a big reprisal raid. No wonder they're losing the bloody war," he added disgustedly.

"They aren't all like that," Armstrong assured him. "Not by any means. So now you've got the green light to go ahead?"

Pittaway nodded. "That's right. Here we are, bombs and all. We've even brought our own armourers with us. We were told to use this airfield because La Vallon is unserviceable for some reason." He half-turned and eyed the airfield. "Looks a bit short to me," he said dubiously. "Still, I expect we'll make it all right. We're only carrying two thousand pounds apiece. At least we won't be faced with a long haul. Some Whitleys flew from the Channel Islands to attack Genoa and Turin a couple of nights ago; the poor buggers were almost asleep in their seats by the time they got back, and to make matters worse they hit sod all and lost an aircraft."

He paused and looked steadily at Armstrong. "Right, then," he said. "What's your excuse?"

Briefly, Armstrong recounted his adventures. Pittaway stared at him with mock awe. "Bloody hell, you certainly get around. I say, are you under anybody's orders? I mean, can you please yourself more or less what you do?"

Armstrong smiled. "Well, I expect orders of various sorts have been chasing me around France, but they haven't caught up with me yet. The Air Ministry has probably written me off. I'll probably be court-martialled when I get back – if I get back."

"In that case, why don't you come on a little tour of northern Italy tonight? Hop aboard, and we'll take a look at Genoa. I might even get my bomb-aimer to let you drop the eggs, if you're very good."

"You're kidding," Armstrong laughed. "I couldn't hit a barn door if I was sitting on the handle. I'd love to come along for the ride, though. By the way, why are you only carrying a two-thousand-pound bomb load? You could have got this far with twice that, couldn't you?"

"Sure we could," Pittaway replied. "It's the bloody politicians again. They reckon with two thousand pounds per aircraft, we can hit the target without much fear of damaging civilian property. With a bigger load, some of the bombs might go astray and kill some Eyeties. Oh, dearie me," he added, rolling his eyes skywards.

Armstrong showed Pittaway where he and his crews could rest and get something to eat, then, still exercising his unofficial role of liaison officer, he went off to see the airfield commandant, who had only learned of the Wellingtons' arrival half an hour before it happened and who was not in the best of humours as a result. Nevertheless, he agreed to institute standing patrols over the airfield until dusk; although the *Regia Aeronautica* had not revisited Luc since its mauling of the previous day, there was nothing to say that it would not do so again. Moreover, both the commandant and Armstrong suspected that there would be Italian agents in the vicinity, their task to report everything that happened at Luc and the other French airfields in the south.

However, the day passed without incident, and a few minutes past midnight found Armstrong sitting in the second pilot's seat of Pittaway's Wellington as it lumbered down the runway between the rows of flares, gathered speed and lifted into the darkness – if it could be called darkness, for even without a moon there was always a translucence about the Mediterranean night, an extra brilliance to the stars that hung over the earth.

The new moon had yet to rise, and so only the stars accompanied the six bombers as they headed out over the coast. The plan was to head due east across the Ligurian Sea to a point north of Corsica, then turn through ninety degrees to approach Genoa from the south. The Italians, Pittaway reasoned, would not be expecting an attack from that direction. Armstrong hoped that his reasoning was correct.

The flight to the turning point was uneventful, except for some scattered anti-aircraft fire that came at them from some ships – probably friendly – and brought forth a string of curses from the crew. Luckily the fire was inaccurate, and soon dwindled astern. Ahead of them now was the coast of Italy, and they had no difficulty at all in locating Genoa.

"Gawd, take a look at that!" Pittaway exclaimed. "It's lit up like a bloody Christmas tree!"

The words were no sooner out of his mouth when the lights went out.

"Thanks a lot, skipper," said the bomb-aimer, from his position in the nose. Normally, the navigator would have dropped the bombs, but on this occasion each Wellington carried an extra crew member; the navigators, Pittaway had reasoned, would probably have their hands full over this unfamiliar territory. After a pause, the bomb-aimer said: "Not to worry, I've got my bearings. Turn left five degrees."

Ahead, the darkness was suddenly split by a searchlight beam. It speared straight up like a luminous finger, remained stationary for a few moments, then began to track to and fro across the sky. It was joined by others, and now the crew could see twinkling flak bursts between the searchlight cones.

"They're a bit premature," Pittaway said laconically.

"Do not jest, skipper," his navigator commented. "Five minutes to target. You okay, George?"

"Yes, I've got it," the bomb-aimer replied. "This heading is fine. Steady as she goes, skipper."

"Roger," Pittaway acknowledged. "Gunners, keep your eyes peeled. There may be fighters about."

"Steady, skipper," the bomb-aimer said again. "We're spot on. I can see the target area. Stand by to drop the flares. Begin descent to five thousand."

Pittaway obeyed the bomb-aimer's instructions. As he levelled out at the required altitude the man in the nose released two flares, which fell into some patchy cloud and shed a soft light over the whole city.

"Marvellous," the bomb-aimer said. "I can see everything. Steady, skipper. Bomb doors open."

The Wellington vibrated as the bomb-bay doors swung down into the slipstream. The other five bombers had dropped back into line astern at half-mile intervals and would now be beginning their individual runs towards the target, guided by the drifting flares.

"Steady, steady . . ." The bomb-aimer's voice sounded unnaturally calm. Looking through the side cockpit window, Armstrong could see the red flashes of anti-aircraft gunfire, but curiously there was no sign of any shellbursts.

165

He wondered why, then realised that the Italian gunners must be firing high, and that the flashes of the bursts were eclipsed by the glare of the searchlights.

"Steady, steady . . . bombs away!" The Wellington gave a leap as the four 500-pound bombs dropped away, and Pittaway's heartfelt comment sounded over the intercom.

"Thank Christ for that! Course for base, nav?"

"Two-five-oh, skipper. Climb to ten thousand."

"Okay. Rear gunner, keep your eye on the target."

"Roger, skip. Oh, there go the bombs. One, two, three – wow! That was a big one. A sort of greenish flash. We've started some fires, by the look of it." His voice took on a sudden note of excitement. "Hello, the searchlights have picked up one of our chaps! He's turning . . . It's okay, they've lost him. There are more bombs exploding. Can't tell if they're on target."

"Right-oh, rear gunner. Well done, everybody. Don't relax, though; we're not out of the wood yet." He glanced across at Armstrong. "Do you mind taking over for a minute, Ken? I could do with a pee."

Armstrong gladly took over the controls, allowing Pittaway to unfasten his seat harness and make his way towards the rear of the fuselage, where there was an Elsan chemical toilet. The Wellington was once again amid the stunning scenery of the Alps. There was little to do now, he told himself, but enjoy the flight back.

He should have known better.

Five miles to the south, a French Potez 631 night fighter was patrolling at roughly the same altitude. Its pilot, *Sergent-Chef* Gillet, was not a happy man. He belonged to one of the French Air Force's five night-fighter *escadrilles*, or rather what was left of it, and he had flown many night patrols since 10 May without seeing a thing. In fact, most of the French night fighters had been used in day combat during the early phase of the campaign, with disastrous results.

On one occasion, eighteen Potez based in the Paris area

had been ordered to attack enemy armoured columns near Fourmies. Six were shot down, and of the others only two – including his own – had returned to their airfields unscathed.

To make matters worse, the Potez, with its twin fins and long cockpit canopy, was often mistaken for the Messerschmitt 110, and several had been shot down by friendly fighters. All in all, the story of the French night fighters had not been a happy one.

Now here Gillet was, flying one of the modified Potez 631s armed with two cannon and seven machine-guns, of which four were fitted under the wings. To compensate for the extra weight a rear gunner was no longer carried, so Gillet was truly a single-seat fighter pilot, a role he had always coveted. It was rather unfortunate, he told himself for the umpteenth time, that he had achieved his ambition when it was too late.

With the battle in the north over, the remnants of Gillet's *escadrille* had been moved to Marseille to provide a defence against the Italian night bombers. That was a laugh! The Italians didn't like flying at night, everyone knew that. They had made not a single night attack; indeed, it seemed they had disappeared from the sky altogether.

Gillet glanced at the luminous dial of the chronometer on his instrument panel. Soon it would be time to return to base at the end of yet another fruitless patrol. He realised that he was still flying east, and tossed a mental coin to decided which way he should turn; north or south. He chose a northerly direction; his intention was to fly towards Monte Viso, then turn south-west towards his base, and some welcome hot coffee.

Suddenly, he frowned. There was something out there ahead of him, something that was not quite right. He strained against his straps, leaning forward to peer through the cockpit windscreen. No, he told himself, he was not mistaken; it was there all right, a black shape skimming between the mountain peaks. An aircraft

– a large aircraft -- crossing into France from enemy territory.

Adrenaline set Gillet's heart pumping as he turned in pursuit of the strange aircraft, releasing the safety-catches of his guns as he did so. He climbed a little so that he was looking down on it, its black silhouette etched on the snow below. Twin engines, a single fin and rudder; it looked a bit like a French Bloch 210 bomber, but it was not. In any case, he knew that they had all been either shot down or grounded through lack of spare parts. So, he asked himself, what were the alternatives?

Gillet was a fairly simple man, and try as he might he couldn't think of any. His reasoning was as simple as his nature. The aircraft was not French, therefore it had to be Italian. The possibility that the RAF might have bombers in this area never once crossed his mind; even if it had, the only British bombers he had seen were Bristol Blenheims and Fairey Battles, neither of which resembled this one.

Carefully, Gillet began to set up his attack.

Pittaway, hugely relieved after his trip to the Elsan, slid back into the first pilot's seat and did up his seat harness, shaking his head when Armstrong asked him if he wanted to take over the controls again. "No, matey, you fly 'er for a bit," he said. "I'm for a coffee." He reached down and pulled a thermos flask from a pouch on the side of the inner fuselage and started to unscrew the lid. "Want some?"

"Wouldn't mind," Armstrong admitted. His throat was dry, and he was chilly.

At that moment, the rear gunner's urgent voice cut across the intercom.

"Skipper, there's an aircraft, working its way around towards our five o'clock position. Can't say what it is. It's not a Wellington, though."

"All right, treat it as hostile and watch it. I want to know every move it makes." Pittaway screwed the cap back on the thermos and stowed the flask in its original position. "Okay, Ken, I'd better take her. You know the drill, though. Stand by to take over if anything happens to me."

"Rear gunner to pilot, the aircraft is turning in. I got quite a good look at it . . . I think it's French, although it looks a bit like an Me 110. Coming round into our six o'clock, now."

"Could be a Potez," Armstrong said doubtfully. "The French have been using some as night fighters."

"Well, keep on watching it like a hawk," Pittaway told the rear gunner. "I don't trust the buggers."

"It's closing in fast," the rear gunner said, his voice high and frightened. "Shall I open fire?"

"Only if it fires first," Pittaway instructed. "If it does, give it all you've got. And stand by for some evasive action."

Holding their breath, they braced themselves.

Chapter Fourteen

In his turret, the rear gunner watched, like a rabbit mesmerised by a stoat, as the dark silhouette of the unidentified fighter grew larger. Suddenly, fire streamed from its nose and wings and red golf balls of tracer shells reached out to ensnare the Wellington. It took him only a fraction of a second to react, and then he too opened fire.

Up front, Armstrong tensed as the red streams of fire ripped past and into the Wellington, and felt rather than heard the vibration as the four Browning .303 machine-guns in the rear turret opened up. Pittaway swore; because of the mountain peaks he was unable to take evasive action laterally, so the only way out was to go either up or down. The trouble was, he couldn't see what lay below.

"Throttles, Ken!" he yelled. Armstrong, understanding what was wanted, opened both throttles wide while Pittaway used both hands to pull back on the control column, putting the bomber into a climb. As he did so, orange flames burst from beneath the starboard engine cowling.

"That's buggered the job," Pittaway gasped. With one engine hit, there would not be enough power to sustain the climb. He eased the pressure on the control column and brought the bomber back to level flight.

At his station further back in the fuselage, the flight engineer hit a button, activating a fire extinguisher that sprayed foam into the crippled engine. For a few seconds the flames dulled and almost died away, then they returned with what seemed renewed intensity.

"Shut it down," Pittaway ordered. The flight engineer

obeyed, using his own bank of throttles to close down the engine, and threw another switch to 'feather' the propeller, turning its blades edge-on to the airflow to reduce the drag.

"Rear gunner, what's the bastard up to now?" Pittaway shouted over the intercom. There was no reply, and Armstrong noticed that the guns had fallen silent. "Nav, go back and find out if he's okay."

A couple of minutes later, the navigator's voice sounded over the intercom. He sounded shaken.

"He's had it, skipper. The turret took a direct hit. He's blown almost in half . . . God, there's blood and guts everywhere."

"All right, spare us the details. Listen, everybody. We can still make it back to base. Nav, get up into the astrodome and watch out for the fighter. Let me know the moment you see him coming in again. Wireless op, get on to the waist guns. On the nav's signal, I'll turn as sharply as I can. See if you can get a shot at the sod."

"Okay, skip." The navigator left his seat and stuck his head into the perspex bubble on top of the fuselage, peering back past the tail fin. "Can't see a thing," he reported a few moments later. "It's the engine fire. There's too much glare. The tail's taken a beating, though. Looks like a lot of loose fabric trailing from it."

"Right. Keep on looking out, anyway." Pittaway glanced across at Armstrong, who at this moment was feeling utterly helpless. "Ken," the New Zealander said, "I'm going to need some help if I have to put her down. She's becoming hard to control."

Armstrong reached out and gripped the control column, following Pittaway's movements. The feel of the stick transferred the bomber's agony to his hands; he could sense the abnormal shuddering and jerking of the control surfaces where shells and bullets had punched through them, the lifting and twisting of the right wing as the good engine did its best to drag the aircraft round towards

171

the left. Adding his strength to Pittaway's, he turned the control column towards the dead motor, lifting the right aileron and lowering the left, allowing the airflow to drop the right wing and so cancel out the bomber's inclination to turn.

A mile astern of the Wellington, *Sergent-Chef* Gillet rolled out of a turn, having broken away after his first firing pass, and went in pursuit of his quarry once more. He had no difficulty in picking it out; the engine he had hit was glowing like a furnace. Keeping the glow centred in his windscreen, he closed in steadily, intent on finishing the job he had begun less than five minutes earlier. This time, he would get in really close.

The glow from the bomber's burning engine grew brighter; sparks and fragments of molten metal swirled past him, and the stench of burning oil pervaded his cockpit. The glow lit up the bomber's camouflage, the code letters and the roundel on its fuselage side.

"The roundel," he whispered to himself in sudden horror. "Oh, my God!"

He could see the colours quite clearly in the glare of the flames. They were red, white and blue. The aircraft was British.

Feeling sick, Gillet pulled off to one side. He had identified the other aircraft now as a Wellington. He began to manoeuvre into position off its port wing, desperately searching his mind for something, anything, he might do to help, some act of atonement to redress his terrible error.

In the astrodome, the navigator saw their attacker for the first time as it crept into position on the starboard beam, and shouted a warning. The wireless operator dashed to the small window in the starboard side of the fuselage and seized the single .303 machine-gun that was mounted there, its position designed to give an arc of fire covering an attack from the beam. Almost at once, he saw the fighter and took careful aim.

"Hold on!" the navigator yelled as he registered what he

172

could see of the other aircraft beyond the roaring torrent of flame from the starboard engine. Its light revealed a roundel to him, too, its colours the reverse of the RAF's. "Hold on! It's French!"

He was too late. In the bomber's waist, the wireless operator took a deep breath and squeezed the trigger, stitching a line of tracer bullets along the full length of the fighter. A couple of seconds was all it took; there was no sign of fire, no sign even that he had hit the other aircraft, but it suddenly dropped away and spiralled down towards the snow-covered crags below.

In the cockpit of the Potez, Gillet registered sudden surprise that he could no longer control his fighter. His hands and feet no longer seemed to obey him. It was all very strange. He had experienced dreams like this; maybe this was a dream. If it wasn't, he could not remember why he was here.

Gillet had not even felt the two bullets that had struck him in the left side. His face was still registering a look of blank amazement when the Potez hit the ground and exploded, but by that time he was dead.

In the Wellington, the wireless operator suddenly realised what the navigator had been shouting. He released his grip on the machine-gun and instead grabbed one of the aluminium bracing spars that formed the bomber's fuselage structure. "Christ," he stammered, "I'm sorry . . . I didn't realise . . ."

Pittaway's crisp tones cut across him. "All right, belt up! Don't worry about it. Crash positions, everybody. It's time to put the old girl down. We're not going to make it back." The bomb-aimer and the front gunner scrambled out of their nose positions and made their way into the main body of the fuselage, leaving Pittaway and Armstrong alone in the front of the aircraft. Suddenly, the New Zealander took a hand off the control column and pointed ahead and down. Peering past the nose, Armstrong saw a broad expanse of snow, nestling between two rock walls. Had there been a moon, casting dark shadows, they might not have recognised it for what it was.

"Looks promising enough," Armstrong commented. "Pretty flat, as far as I can tell."

"Well, old son, we don't have much choice, do we?" Pittaway observed.

Armstrong didn't need to voice his agreement. Pittaway was already throttling back the engine that was still running, at the same time pointing the Wellington's nose towards the plateau. Anxiously, Armstrong looked out of the side window at the flames that were now eating into the wing; it would be touch and go whether they would get down before the fire reached a fuel tank. Every second was precious now.

"Ken, I have control. Stand by to drop the flaps when I tell you."

Armstrong relinquished his hold on the control column and placed his hand on the flap lever. The snowfield was coming up at them rapidly now; Pittaway chopped the throttle and the port engine fell silent, its propeller windmilling. Behind the pilots' positions, the flight engineer hurriedly flicked off all the engine and fuel control switches and turned his seat to face rearwards, tightening his harness.

"Here we go," Pittaway said calmly. "Flaps! Brace, brace, brace!"

Armstrong pulled hard on the flap lever and the Wellington's nose lifted a little as the flaps bit into the airflow, decelerating the big bomber in the final stage of its descent. It seemed to hang motionless for long seconds, the only sounds the sigh of the airflow and the roar and crackle from the burning engine. Then its belly struck the snow.

Armstrong had been expecting a massive impact. Instead, there was only the slightest rumble, followed by a series of minor jolts. Snow flew back in a spray over the leading edges of the wings. The bomber careered on like a toboggan, sliding on its underside, with no apparent deceleration. Ice particles obscured the windscreen, blocking the view ahead. Pittaway and Armstrong stared at the opaque layer, transfixed. The New Zealander was instinctively juggling with the controls, even though he was utterly powerless to check the Wellington's long slide.

Then the bomber's left wingtip hit an outcrop of rock, and the noise and disintegration began. With a jolt that rattled every bone, the Wellington slewed round through ninety degrees, shedding lumps of wing as it went. It continued to slide sideways, but then the starboard wing dug itself in and the headlong momentum began to fall away. Then, with a hideous screeching and rending, the wing broke up. The section outboard of the still-burning engine folded up and spun away into the darkness, and then the engine itself tore from its mountings, rupturing fuel and oil lines and the walls of the petrol tank embedded in the wing's inner section.

With a huge thud and a series of metallic crunches, the Wellington came to a sudden stop. The pilots' seat harnesses bit painfully into their upper bodies as they were hurled brutally forward, but mercifully the straps held. From somewhere in the fuselage there came a cry of pain.

Then, for long moments, there was a deep silence, broken only by laboured breathing and the cracking of twisted metal. Armstrong registered everything through a stunned daze, and shook his head to clear it. Automatically, he fumbled for the release of his seat harness. He was dimly conscious of a red glare shining through the cockpit window on his side.

Pittaway punched him sharply on the arm, bringing him fully to his senses, or almost. Armstrong looked at his companion groggily.

"Come on, quick!" Pittaway shouted, his voice echoing strangely. "She's going to go up – there's fuel all over the place! Let's get the others out."

They clambered unsteadily from their seats, flexing themselves to see if they were still in one piece, and made their way back into the main fuselage. Someone had already kicked out one of the glazed side panels, and a stream of icy air was swirling into the aircraft. One by one, the other crew members scrambled out into the night, urging each other on. Pittaway pushed Armstrong in the same direction, took a last look around the interior to make certain that no one was left behind, then followed suit.

Ahead of him, Armstrong stepped out onto the wing, which was half buried in snow, and slid off it onto a surface which was surprisingly firm. Although he was wearing a flying overall, with a fur-lined jacket on top of it, knife-edged cold struck him like a physical blow. A sudden thought flashed through his mind and he stumbled around the rear of the aircraft, past the shattered turret with the remains of the rear gunner still trapped inside, towards the lurid glare that formed the only light in an otherwise darkened wilderness.

On the opposite side of the Wellington he came to a sudden stop, appalled by the damage the aircraft had suffered. The engine lay some distance away, in the middle of a pool of burning petrol; there was a good deal of spilt fuel near the wreck, too, but there was no sign of the flames extending to it. He made a closer inspection to ensure that his first impression was correct, then went back to rejoin the others. All five of them were safe, apart from some cuts and bruises, although the navigator had taken a nasty blow to the head. It was his cry they had heard.

"It's all right," Armstrong informed Pittaway. "I don't think the aircraft is in any danger from the fire. It's dying down, anyway." He shivered; the iciness of the night seemed to be growing more intense.

"Look," he said, "there's nothing we can do until it's light. I suggest we get back into the fuselage and unpack the parachutes; the canopies will make good insulation. For God's sake, though, don't anyone light a cigarette!"

"What about him?" the wireless operator asked, indicating the rear turret and its grim burden.

"There's nothing we can do for him," Pittaway said. "Come on, let's get back inside. It'll be dawn in about three hours. We might as well make ourselves as comfortable as we can, and try to get some rest."

They clambered back into the wreck of the bomber and set to work pulling the ripcords of their parachutes, allowing the silk to spill out inside the fuselage. As Armstrong had predicted, it protected them from the worst of the cold, although the temperature was still low enough to deny them anything more than a fitful doze.

It was a vast relief when daylight came. The bomb-aimer was the first to venture outside, intent on answering the call of nature. A moment later they heard him give a howl: "Christ, but it's cold!" His comment brought the amusement they all sorely needed.

Armstrong and the others followed the bomb-aimer outside. As he had proclaimed, it was cold all right, but not as freezing as Armstrong had expected.

Their first task, before taking stock of their situation, was to drape a parachute over the rear gun turret. Although they were only too aware of what was in it, at least now they would not have to look at the unfortunate gunner's remains.

The Wellington had come to rest perilously close to the western edge of the plateau, at the end of a long swathe of churned-up snow. While the others broke into their emergency rations and set about preparing a meal of sorts, Armstrong and Pittaway walked back along the track the Wellington had made, their faces turned to the rising sun, visible now as a heatless red ball between two mountains.

"Well, we know where we are," Pittaway remarked. A few minutes earlier, the navigator had managed to pinpoint their position on the map by reference to the surrounding mountains and valleys. Technically, their wrecked bomber was just inside French territory. "The problem is, we don't know whether this bit of the Alps is still in French hands, or whether the French have pulled out."

"Well, we should know soon enough," Armstrong said. "Somebody is certain to be out looking for us." He grabbed Pittaway suddenly by the arm. "In fact," he continued, lowering his voice as though in fear of being overheard, "I think that somebody has passed this way already."

He pointed at some marks in the snow. They were ski tracks, and there were a lot of them. As far as the two pilots could tell, they crossed the plateau in a straight line from north to south. Pittaway crouched down to examine them.

"Hm. A day or two old, maybe. Both sides must have outposts up here. There'll be regular patrols, I expect." He looked up at the encircling peaks, then back at the tracks. "Do you think we ought to follow them?"

"No, I don't," Armstrong said decisively, shaking his head. "If anyone up here was even half awake last night, they'll have seen us coming down for miles around. We were pretty well lit up, after all. They'll be looking for us, you can bet on it."

"I suppose you're right," the New Zealander admitted. "Come on, let's get some breakfast. If the wrong lot gets to us first, we could end up munching spaghetti for the foreseeable future."

Breakfast, culled from the survival rations, was bully beef, hardtack biscuits, chocolate and boiled sweets, washed down with the most welcome brew of tea Armstrong had ever tasted, or so it seemed at the time, brought to the boil on a small primus stove. As they ate, Pittaway explained to the others what he and Armstrong had found, and outlined the various possibilities that confronted them.

"Can't we walk out, sir?" the wireless operator wanted to know, when Pittaway asked if anyone had any questions. The pilot shook his head.

"Out of the question. It might be okay during the day, but without proper shelter we'd freeze to death at night.

Stay with the aircraft, that's the golden rule. We've got food, we've got water" – he waved a hand at the snow that surrounded them – "and we'll be easy to spot from the air. Don't forget that our other crews probably saw us go down, so they'll have raised the alarm. All we have to do is sit tight, and wait to be rescued."

It was mid-morning when they sighted the aircraft, heading directly towards them from the east. On Pittaway's order they piled back into the wrecked Wellington; the New Zealander wanted to be certain what it was that was bearing down on them before they revealed themselves. He peered cautiously up through the astrodome as the aircraft flew overhead and then turned back to circle the spot, and then beckoned to Armstrong.

"Come up and take a look, Ken. What do you make of it?"

Armstrong surveyed the aircraft as it made a run overhead. It was a single-engined biplane with a spatted undercarriage. He was certain that it was Italian, less certain what type it was. "I think it's an Ro 37," he said hesitantly, wishing his knowledge of Italian aircraft was as thorough as it was of German types. "An observation aircraft. Hello – looks as though he has seen enough." The biplane, having made a couple of orbits over the plateau, flew off the way it had come.

"We can expect visitors, then," Pittaway grunted. "Well, we'll give 'em a warm reception. Come on—let's get the two beam guns unshipped, with as much ammo as possible. We'll set up a couple of positions at the far end of the plateau."

It took them an hour to complete the task. Using the emergency axe from the aircraft, they dug foxholes in the ice and insulated them with parachute silk, which they also used as makeshift camouflage to make their positions invisible from the air. The snow on the plateau was as hard as concrete, and there were no telltale footprints that might give them away.

179

Pittaway was convinced that help would reach them that day, and that it was simply a matter of keeping the Italians at arm's length until it arrived. Their positions commanded a fine view of the defile that led up to the southern edge of the plateau, and the two air gunners seemed confident that they could pin down anyone who came that way. The six men settled down for what might turn out to be a long, cold wait.

After a couple of hours, the distant drone of an aero-engine heralded the reappearance of the Italian observation aircraft. It passed directly overhead, circled the wrecked Wellington once, and then flew back down the defile. They saw it waggle its wings, as though signalling to someone on the ground, and then it turned around the side of a mountain and disappeared from view.

"Can't see anything down there," Pittaway said, cautiously peering down the defile from under a fold of parachute silk. He called softly to the men in the adjacent foxhole, which was sited a few yards away. "Any sign of life?"

There was a pause, then one of the gunners called back: "I'm not quite sure, skipper, but I think I can see some movement . . . Yes, they're there all right. You see those rocky outcrops that look a bit like a cat's claws? There's a patrol coming round them. Ten men, maybe a dozen. About a mile away, I reckon."

"Yes, I can see 'em now. Okay, let's let 'em get really close. Wait for my word, then let 'em have it."

Next to Pittaway, Armstrong checked his Smith and Wesson .38 Service revolver. He hoped he would not have to use it. He had never killed a man face to face, and didn't relish the prospect. But he knew that if he had to do it, he would.

The enemy troops came on at a steady pace, methodically working their way up the defile. Armstrong felt sorry for them. The crew of the observation aircraft must have indicated that the wrecked bomber was deserted, that the

180

survivors, if there were any, had decided to walk out. The Italians were laughing and joking amongst themselves as they plodded on; they obviously had no inkling of what lay ahead of them.

Pittaway let them get to within less than a hundred yards, then gave the order to open fire.

Chapter Fifteen

The rattle of the two machine-guns was shockingly loud, magnified by the echoes that rebounded from the surrounding mountains. The bullets cut into the Italian soldiers, hurling them to the ground in a welter of blood. Some died without knowing what had hit them; others writhed in the reddening snow, screaming in shock and pain, until the bullets traversed to and fro across them and silenced them forever.

Then there were only the echoes, and a ringing silence. Armstrong looked at the carnage and felt sick. So, judging by their expressions, did the others.

"Poor bastards," Pittaway murmured. "Still, it had to be done."

"Hold on, skip. Look. Look there." Pittaway looked at where the gunner who had spoken was pointing. More men were emerging from behind the rocky outcrop. As he watched, they suddenly went to ground, alerted by the sound of gunfire. They would be able to see what had happened to their comrades, and Armstrong had an unpleasant feeling that they would not be in the mood to take prisoners, if it came to that.

"I wish we had some binoculars," Pittaway said. "I think they're up to something. Can't see what, though. Do you reckon they can see us?"

Armstrong shook his head. "Don't think so. But they'll know roughly where we are by just looking at the bodies. My guess is . . ."

What Armstrong's guess was, nobody ever found out.

His words were interrupted by a dull thump from where the Italians were sheltering behind their rocks. A black object curved high over the defile, reached the top of its trajectory, then descended towards them, gathering speed as gravity helped it on its way.

"Mortar bomb!" Pittaway yelled. "Get down, everybody!"

Six heads vanished into the foxholes as the bomb plunged down, emitting a shrill whistle. Seconds later, it exploded below the edge of the plateau, close to where the dead Italians lay. Powdered snow pattered down on the foxholes, bringing with it a strong stench of explosives.

A second thud told the airmen that another bomb was on its way, and they ducked down once more. This time, the missile exploded a short distance away, right on the rim of the plateau. A third impacted just behind them.

"Time to leave," Pittaway shouted. "Grab the guns and ammo and get back to the aircraft. Get a move on!"

They abandoned their positions and ran back to the wrecked bomber. As they did so, more mortar bombs exploded behind them, on and around the foxholes they had just vacated. It had been a close thing, Armstrong told himself, and wondered what Pittaway was going to do now. Whichever way you looked at it, he thought, they were pretty well snookered; the Italians could make a quick recce of the plateau, see how the land lay, stay out of sight and lob mortar bombs over. There was nowhere to go; nowhere to hide. If they stayed together near the Wellington the bombs would get them; if they split up and made a run for it their hope of rescue would vanish like morning mist.

"We'll make a stand over there," Pittaway said. "Between the western edge of the plateau and the Wellington. The Eyeties will think we've taken shelter in the aircraft, and with a bit of luck they'll use up their mortar bombs on it. When they come up over the far side of the plateau, we'll use up the rest of our ammo on them and then scarper. It's the best we can do."

Closer to the edge of the plateau there were some ridges of rough ice, big enough to hide the airmen. They took shelter behind them, getting the machine-guns ready for action again and taking stock of their remaining ammunition. It was one thing they had in plenty; they hauled more from the wreck of the Wellington and the gunners surrounded themselves with belts of it. Then, once again, they waited.

They could feel the warmth of the sun now, although it was not strong enough to melt the snow on the plateau. It was a hell of a way to visit some of the world's most picturesque scenery, Armstrong thought. See the Alps and die. Well, it was as good a place as any.

Half an hour went by; threequarters. There was no sign of any activity on the far side of the plateau, although the Italians must surely have reached it by now. They must be hatching some sort of plan, something foolproof that would avoid further losses.

"Hullo," Pittaway said, "our little friend is coming back." He pointed towards a speck in the eastern sky.

"There's more than one," someone else remarked. It was one of the air gunners, who had exceptionally keen eyesight. He was right; within a few moments, Armstrong was able to count four incoming aircraft. A few moments more, and he was able to identify them. They were Fiat G.50 monoplane fighters, distinctive by virtue of their raised cockpits, which gave them a hump-backed appearance.

As he and the others watched, the fighters dropped into a line-astern formation, the roar of their radial engines swelling as they went into a shallow dive, heading directly for the plateau. "Looks as though they mean mischief," Pittaway said. "Take cover, everybody!"

The men flattened themselves in their foxholes, trying to make themselves as inconspicuous as possible. "Don't

184

shoot at them!" Pittaway yelled. "The troops will be coming in next—save your ammo for them!"

His words were drowned by the leading Fiat, which flattened out a few feet above the plateau, its machine-guns chattering as the pilot opened fire on the wreck of the Wellington. The fighter flashed overhead and the second attacked in turn. Bullets ricocheted off the ice and howled off into the distance. The third and fourth aircraft came in, and this time their gunfire produced a flicker of flame from the bomber's port wing. It died away, then reappeared more strongly as the fighters climbed away and turned to make a second run. Their bullets, Armstrong realised, had found their mark in the Wellington's wing tank, which was still intact and must now be filled with volatile petrol vapour. At this altitude, with a reduced oxygen content in the atmosphere, it was taking a few seconds longer than normal to ignite.

As the leading Fiat turned in again, the fuel tank suddenly erupted with a dull roar. One by one, the Italian fighters sprayed more bullets into the smoke that burgeoned up. The wreck was well alight now, the flames spreading rapidly to engulf the fuselage, soon creating a funeral pyre for the luckless rear gunner. Ammunition that remained in the bomber started to explode, sending a pyrotechnic display of tracer high into the air.

The fourth and last Fiat sped through the spreading pall of smoke and flew past the spot where the six airmen were sheltering. As it did so, it dipped a wing towards them before climbing away. There was no doubt that its pilot had seen them. All of them watched it as it curved up past the mountainside, showing its mottled upper surfaces, following the three ahead.

It exploded.

There was no warning. One moment the Italian fighter was there, its sleek lines resplendent in the sunlight. The next it was a ball of debris, bouncing and fragmenting down the mountain slope, leaving a trail of blazing fuel in its wake.

A Curtiss Hawk sped past the flaming wreck, followed by three more, heading to intercept the other Fiats. The six airmen looked up as more aircraft thundered overhead: Dewoitines this time, skimming over the plateau and disappearing beyond it. The bark of their 20-mm cannon joined the rattle of their machine-guns as they pounded the unseen Italian troops. Armstrong and the others jumped to their feet, shouting and waving, clapping one another on the back as they watched the D.520s rocket up in a climb, looking like dark toys against the background of the far mountain slopes.

Armstrong looked in the opposite direction and gave a yell, pointing. Threading its way through the pass on the western side of the plateau was a twin-engined, low-wing monoplane. At first Armstrong thought that it was an Airspeed Oxford, an RAF trainer, but then he recognised it for what it was: a Potez 56 civil airliner. He had glimpsed it on the airfield at Luc, being worked on by an Air France crew.

The Potez pilot throttled back, his engines burbling as he touched down as close as possible to the western edge of the plateau to give himself plenty of room. The small airliner's undercarriage crunched on the hard-packed snow. The aircraft rolled on past Armstrong and the others, skidding a little, but the pilot controlled its landing run skilfully. It stopped in an amazingly short distance, just beyond the smoke from the burning Wellington, then turned in a large and cautious circle until it was facing into wind again, close to where the six were waiting. A side cockpit window opened and a head poked out.

"Come on, get in. I haven't got all bloody day," shouted Stanislaw Kalinksi, in his heavily accented English.

EPILOGUE

"God, what a homecoming."

Armstrong stared at the Liverpool skyline, shrouded in drizzle. The others – Kalinski and the Poles, Pittaway and his crew – were spread out along the destroyer's rail.

"Oh, I dunno," the New Zealander commented. "It's good to be back."

They had been among the last personnel to be evacuated from the south of France, on the day the anticipated armistice had come into effect. Most of the French pilots had flown their aircraft to North Africa; the Poles, to a man, had elected to come to England. The French had fought gallantly to the bitter end, but it had been hopeless. Hopeless ever since, weeks earlier, France's politicians had lost the will to fight.

But there were Frenchmen who would fight on; Armstrong was sure of that. British, French, Poles, Belgians, Czechs, Dutch, Norwegians – a bond of nations strengthened by their first-hand experience of the evil that had descended on the continent of Europe.

There remained a small offshore island, facing the direst challenge in a thousand years of its history. Armstrong knew, they all knew, that the great battle to come, the battle upon which Britain's survival and the fate of the free world depended, would be fought and decided in the air.

Pittaway tapped him on the arm. He looked up, and saw a pair of purposeful, shark-like aircraft drop down through the drizzle. The Spitfires flew low past the destroyer as it continued its passage through Liverpool

Bay, then disappeared inland, their outlines blurred by the rain.

Yes, thought Armstrong, Pittaway was right. It was good to be back.